FOREVER HER DUKE

DUKES MOST WANTED
BOOK ONE

SCARLETT SCOTT

Happily Ever After Books

Forever Her Duke

Dukes Most Wanted Book One

For Steve ~ Thank you for always supporting me, for making me laugh with your ridiculousness, and for being my everything.

CHAPTER 1

The carriage ambling up the winding approach of Sherborne Manor was too early to be carrying Lady Clementine Hammond. Vivi was in the gardens when she first spied it, directing the head gardener on the final plans for the life-size chessboard she wished to be constructed on the north lawn.

"The squares must be painted, not powdered, Shipley," she said, frowning from beneath the brim of her straw hat as she watched the mysterious carriage's slow progression. "I want it to resemble a chessboard as closely as you can possibly manage, but we also need to consider the necessity of keeping our lady guests' hems from being soiled."

Soiled hems simply would *not* do at a house party being held by the Duchess of Bradford. She had a reputation to uphold, after all. Vivi went to extraordinary lengths to make certain her guests left her every fête with a smile and a sigh over how wonderfully delightful even the smallest detail had been.

The food was always the finest to be served, the guests in attendance were hand-chosen by Vivi and certain to be witty and amusing, and every facet, from the flowers to the entertainments to the beating of the carpets, was carefully and strategically plotted and overseen by Vivi herself.

"Of course, Your Grace," Shipley said agreeably. "I wouldn't dream of powdering the lawn."

"I'm relieved to hear it," she said distractedly, for the carriage was drawing nearer, and from her vantage point in the gardens, she recognized the familiar crest on the door. What in heaven's name was her mother-in-law doing, arriving at Sherborne Manor when Vivi was about to host the grandest house party she had held yet? "Please also see the roses are cut and delivered to the main house for placement the morning my guests first begin arriving. I want the blossoms to be fresh, so be sure to select tightly furled buds rather than flowers in full bloom. The mess of dropping petals is so very disagreeable."

"I'll be certain to send only the best buds, Your Grace," the head gardener reassured her.

She had no reason to require the reassurance. She knew Shipley was an incredibly competent fellow, for she had hired him herself in her husband's extended absence, the gardens having been left overgrown and in abysmal condition. Over the past year, and under her guidance, the gardens had been painstakingly restored to their former glory. But this house party was important to Vivi. Incredibly important, and she wanted everything to be perfect.

Which was why she needed to address the arrival of that blasted carriage.

"Thank you, Shipley," she said, offering him a smile. "I am a confident hostess with you at the helm of the Sherborne Manor gardens. Now, I must attend to some other matters."

The head gardener bowed. "Of course, Your Grace."

Vivi's feet were moving, carrying her through the gardens toward the main house. She had spent the morning in boots and a serviceable day gown with her old straw hat—secretly her favorite attire. The boots were broken in and the gown worn and soft from overuse, her hat ten years out of style and quite a monstrosity, its massive brim perfect for keeping the sun from making freckles appear on her forehead and nose.

Ordinarily, she wouldn't greet the august lady in such an undignified state. But the carriage was gliding toward the front portico now, out of sight, and she needed to stop the dowager before she became too settled and inform her mother-in-law that a house party was about to begin. The dowager detested social gatherings.

Heavens, the dowager detested people. Vivi would never know how the woman could have produced a son as gregarious and magnetic and smoothly charming as Court. Although she was a woman grown of six and-twenty, the dowager never failed to make Vivi feel as if she were a girl in short skirts, in need of remonstration and the iron rule of a stern governess.

What would she do if her mother-in-law insisted on remaining as a guest? They would have a veritable thundercloud looming over the entire affair, creating a pall not even the fine delicacies her chef cooked up, nor the endless entertainments she had devised, would lift.

It would be an unmitigated disaster.

Vivi's feet flew faster. She slipped in a side door and hastened to the entry hall, praying she wouldn't be too late.

A flurry of *Your Graces* reached her as the tattered hem of her old gray gown swished about her boots and her soles clicked on the polished parquet. She stopped to find the housekeeper, Mrs. Porritt, approaching with a chatelaine jingling at her waist. On her heels was the chambermaid who had been directed to oversee the cleaning of all the bedchambers in the west wing.

Suppressing a sigh, Vivi turned her attention toward the capable housekeeper first, in deference to her position. "Yes, Mrs. Porritt?"

"Shall I have the duke's bedchamber aired out and freshened, Your Grace?" the housekeeper asked.

The duke? Her husband, the duke? The man she hadn't seen in a year? The man whom she had loved since she'd been but a girl meeting her older brother Percy's school chum for the first time?

If only.

But no, she had abandoned the hope that the man she had married would ever return to her. Court had left the morning after their wedding day, bidding her farewell when she had only just returned from a morning ride, and as far as she knew, he had yet to come back to England. As the tales of his adventures—complete with scandal and dubious associations with other women—had reached her, she had been forced to concede it was entirely possible the man she had loved had been nothing but a chimera. He was as lost to her now as Percy was.

"Of course not, Mrs. Porritt," she declined, tamping down the accompanying sadness at the thought of her beloved brother. "His Grace is not in residence here at Sherborne Manor, as you know. Such an effort won't be necessary."

"But, Your Grace—" the staid housekeeper protested in an unusual show of persistence.

"Not now, if you please," Vivi interrupted, turning toward the chambermaid, ever cognizant of the arriving carriage and the need to address it and its occupant both. "Lumley, what do you require?"

"The green bedchamber appears to have water damage, Your Grace," the maid said, her gaze darting between Vivi and the housekeeper. "A spring storm brought down one of the old trees in the garden, and the branches must have punctured the roof. One of the girls has been to the attic, she has, and reports a fair bit of damage above, as well as the plaster below in the guest room."

"Not the green chamber," she muttered, for it was where she had been intent upon placing the meddling Marchioness of Featherstone. "How bad is it, Lumley?"

"I'm sure I couldn't say the extent for myself, Your Grace," Lumley said, lowering her head with humility. "Perhaps Mrs. Porritt or Mr. Alderson might know better than I myself would."

A new sound reached Vivi as she grappled with the unwanted news concerning the green chamber—it was the centuries' old front door swinging open and then closing again.

The dowager had already arrived.

She was *inside* the house.

Perish the thought.

Vivi took a deep breath, then exhaled, steeling herself for a confrontation with her mother-in-law, who had never failed to make her disapproval of—and eternal disappointment in—Vivi well-known. For she believed Vivi was responsible for Court's defection. And in a sense, she was not wrong. However, what Vivi had never swallowed her pride enough to reveal to the dowager was that she would have given anything to keep her husband at her side. How she had needed him in those early days, Percy's death still so fresh, his absence in her life a wound that still had yet to heal. And how Court's leaving had torn her apart, as mercilessly as any blade.

"I will return in a moment, Mrs. Porritt, Lumley," she said.

Leaving the servants in her wake, Vivi reached the end of the hall leading to the great entry.

And promptly stopped, shock rendering her motionless.

For there, in the marble-floored entry to Sherborne Manor, with its trickling Poseidon fountain hidden in an alcove gurgling merrily away and its hideous spoils of previous Dukes of Bradford mounted all over the walls in dubious array, stood not the dowager Duchess of Bradford as Vivi had feared.

But rather, a far more perplexing creature: a man who was vexingly tall and broad of shoulder, long-legged and lean-hipped and undeniably dangerous-looking. His dark hair was nearly long enough to brush his shoulders, a well-trimmed beard shadowing his jaw. She had a vague impression of sharp cheekbones above the beard and startling green-blue eyes.

Disturbingly familiar eyes.

She stopped, the world spinning about her.

And then the unexpected arrival spoke. "Hullo, Vivi."

That voice.

She would recognize it anywhere, for it was the voice of Harcourt Sherborne, the Duke of Bradford, the man she had loved ever since she had been fourteen years old and he had been a lofty eighteen. He had given her a grin and his most courtly bow, and he had stolen her heart forever.

Her *husband.*

CHAPTER 2

*H*is wife.

Court stood in the hall of his own country seat for the first time in too damned long, feeling like a bloody intruder as he stared at the woman before him.

He suddenly felt every one of his thirty years. Much had altered during his absence. And it was more than apparent to him now as he stared at her, awe combining with a curious sensation in his chest, that the tearful bride he had left behind had turned into a formidable woman whilst he had been gone.

A duchess in her own right, even if she was wearing a bedraggled gray gown and a floppy-brimmed straw hat. Perversely, the sight of her with such a shocking lack of polish—the opposite of every sharp-tongued letter he had received from his mother in his travels—filled him with a new sense of appreciation.

A very male and primitive one. But that, too, filled him with old guilt. For this was Vivi. His best friend's younger sister, the one whom he had promised he would never touch. The girl who had swum in the lake in her shift and caught

7

frogs in her bare hands and fished with him and Percy when they'd been lads up from Eton. She was also the wild hoyden he'd married in the darkest depths of his grief over Percy's death.

When last he'd seen her, her nose had been dappled with freckles, her boots had been caked in mud, and she'd just returned from riding her favorite horse, Visigoth, like the wind.

"Vivi," he repeated, the pet name Percy had always used for her.

A pet name he had been granted permission to use for her as well in those careless days.

He and Vivi had been friends, great friends, once. And then one reckless night had quite thoroughly ruined that. Or perhaps, to be more accurate, *he* had quite thoroughly ruined that. He had missed her every moment he had been gone, but he hadn't realized just how much until he stood here on the great hall marble, busts of Dukes of Bradford past watching on with censorious stares.

Her shoulders went back, spine stiffening, and she snatched the hat from her head, leaving the small golden curls framing her face in disarray. The color of her hair—bright and pale as wheat in the sun—had not altered, even if the way she looked at him had.

"What are you doing here, Bradford?" she demanded curtly, thoroughly dashing the foolish musings. "I thought you were in Paris."

She had not called him Court, he noted, but Bradford, the appellation and mantle he loathed, more suited to his odious sire than to himself. Moreover, he had last been in Paris months ago. Most recently, he had been in New York City. He wondered if she bothered to read the letters he sent her.

It shouldn't matter either way; he was the one who had gone away. And yet, he couldn't shake the acute stab of disappointment knifing through him at the notion that all his efforts to connect with her from afar might have been thoroughly ignored. But then, he should have expected as much, for he had never received a response from her. The silence, like the time and the distance, had simply lagged on, until he'd reached the end of his self-imposed exile, and the strain from being away from her had proven too much.

He summoned a forced smile. "I was under the impression this was my home. Am I not welcome here?"

Court cursed himself for the touch of bitterness leaching into the question. There was something damned disagreeable in the air here at Sherborne Manor. It was as if all the agony and despair of centuries' worth of miserable Sherborne ancestors had seeped into the stone foundation, remaining like wraiths to haunt the unfortunates who still traversed these halls.

He hated it here. He should not have come. Would not have done, were it not where his wife was. *His wife.* Christ, but it felt strange and yet right to call her that. To look upon her and think something so ridiculously possessive as *mine*. He hated himself for the awareness of her careening through him. For the thoughts of her beauty, for the unwanted longing.

What would Percy say if he could see his oldest chum now? Court shuddered to think it.

Vivi was frowning at him as if he were the source of her everlasting disappointment. She had not moved any nearer, making no effort to close the distance between them. Nor to greet him in a wifely manner.

Not even a friendly one.

His wife's blue eyes were fashioned of ice.

"Of course you are welcome," she said, her tone of voice suggesting entirely the opposite.

Court was vaguely aware of some female domestics

hovering in the distance, one of whom appeared to be matronly and elegantly dressed enough to be the housekeeper his wife had hired according to his steward, a set of keys hanging at her waist. They had an audience. He ought to keep his thoughts to himself.

And yet, his stupid mouth was moving. Moving the same way his legs were, carrying him closer to the wife he had missed.

"You are not pleased to see me," he observed, stopping before her.

The freckles were gone, he realized, mourning their charming path which had once reminded him of a constellation all her own lightly dancing over the delicate bridge of her nose. He wondered what else had changed. What she had lost besides the tiny coppery specks that had once entranced him.

"You are unexpected, Your Grace," she said with cold civility.

Decidedly not the spirited hoyden he remembered. She had a smear of dirt on her cheekbone, and he longed to wipe it from her pale skin. Perhaps there was a hint of her former self lingering within, the intrepid girl whose bravery and determination had never ceased to amaze him.

"Formality, Vivi?" he asked, an odd, hurt sensation lingering, rather like an old wound newly opened.

Like Percy's death.

Like returning to England and being forced to face the fact that his friend was no longer here. How easy it had been by comparison, to travel and lie to himself that Percy was merely at home in England. That he hadn't drowned when the *Marguerite* had been swallowed by the sea.

Vivi's full lips tightened incrementally, and Court couldn't help but notice how full and lush they were, the pale, delicate pink of a summer rose in bloom. Lips he remembered beneath his all too well.

"How am I meant to greet a stranger, if not with formality?" she asked, her voice dripping with scorn.

She was angry with him.

He might have known; indeed, he had brought it on himself, keeping his distance for so long.

"I'm hardly a stranger," he reminded her. "You've known me since you were a girl who adored splashing in puddles and climbing trees."

She remained unsmiling and aloof, staring at him with an inscrutable gaze that may as well have been a blade for the way it cut at him. "I realized some time ago that I never knew you, Bradford. Now, if you please, tell me what you are doing here and when you plan to leave again. I have dozens of guests about to descend upon me in two weeks' time, and your unexpected arrival only adds to the strain of the household preparations."

She made him feel unwelcome. As if he were an undesirable visitor in his own home. Never mind that it was a home he never had truly felt comfortable in; it was the ancestral estate that reminded him of his father, the previous Duke of Bradford, a man who had been as unforgiving as he had been cold and cruel.

"Dozens of guests?" he repeated, focusing on that detail rather than the sharp rebuke unspoken in her words. "What is the reason for it?"

"The reason?" Her nostrils flared—a small characteristic he recalled from their younger days, whenever he had bested her at something.

Somehow, it pleased him to see this old part of herself, regardless that it meant she was irritated with him. He had earned her irritation, after all. But he wouldn't think of all the ways he had failed her and Percy just now.

"Yes, the reason, Vivi dear," he explained patiently, still distracted by that errant smudge of dirt on her delicate cheekbone, which seemed to call for him to remove it, though he dared not touch her. Not yet, even if his heart demanded the contact he'd spent all his time away pining for. "Why should you have dozens of guests about to arrive at Sherborne Manor?"

And how soon would they be leaving? He hadn't intended to have a damned audience for his wooing. It would be awkward enough attempting to make amends for the past without being presided over by London lords and ladies, sharp-tongued gossips, and stiff-backed sticklers for propriety alike.

His wife didn't answer his question, however. Instead, she spun on her heel and strode away from him. There was a swing to her hips that was all womanly, and the ankles peeping from the dampened hem of her gown were well-turned and tempting. Her waist was as lush as he remembered, the pleasing curves calling for his hands to travel over them, to learn her shape anew.

To relearn her as a woman.

He felt it suddenly again, an irresistible pull of attraction for her. He hadn't wanted it when they had married, for it had felt like a betrayal.

His distraction over his wife's womanly shape ended as she turned back to him, having seized a large vase of freshly cut flowers from a nearby table covered in bric-a-brac. Why in the devil had she decided to fetch it in the midst of their discussion?

"I am expecting guests," she hissed quietly, her eyes flashing with icy fire, "because I am hosting a house party. A house party you neither know about nor were invited to because you have spent the past year flitting about the world like a bachelor instead of a man with a wife."

With that stinging admonition, she pulled back the vase and emptied it, water, flowers, and all, upon him.

Cold liquid splashed in his eyes and rolled down his cheeks, dripping over his shirtfront and progressing along his trousers to his booted feet. He stood there in a state of shock, too surprised to move. Too muttonheaded to have defended himself.

"And do not," growled the girl whose braids he had once tugged, "ever again call me *Vivi dear.*"

CHAPTER 3

*C*ourt was home.

Vivi's hands were shaking.

She could scarcely credit that the husband who had abandoned her and spent the last year traveling the world alone had returned. Fortunately, her dear friend Clementine had planned an early arrival at Sherborne Manor. On account of her unwanted visitor's disturbing presence, Vivi had decided to journey to the train station herself to meet Clementine rather than merely sending the coachman as planned.

Anything to escape Court's unsettling presence.

"You are overset," her friend observed, frowning at her as the carriage took them from the bustle of the train station.

Vivi had blurted the dreadful news of the duke's return to Lady Clementine the moment they had entered the private confines of the vehicle. As it was, she felt perilously close to tears.

She twisted her fingers in the fall of her silk skirts. "Of course I am. It is an unmitigated disaster."

"I thought you had missed him," her friend said quietly.

She *had* missed him. Terribly. That was part of the problem. Court being gone for so long had been the most devastating blow Vivi had been dealt aside from losing Percy. In a way, his abandonment had been like a second death. He had broken her heart. Crushed it to infinitesimal little bits and then ground those bits into dust before flinging them to the wind whilst he sailed off to dally with light-skirts and forget her existence.

But she wouldn't think about those terrible rumors now.

"It doesn't signify whether I missed him," she snapped, feeling peevish and raw, all her emotions churning uncontrollably within her. "I don't want him here now. Not after everything that's happened, and most especially not with the house party I have been planning so carefully about to begin in a fortnight. Only think of what Lady Featherstone will tell everyone."

"Lady Featherstone is attending?" Clementine shuddered "I hope Charity doesn't know that. She is convinced the marchioness is responsible for the whispers surrounding her about the Venus portrait. She'll likely invent an excuse not to attend and run off to the Continent."

Lady Charity Manners was another dear friend in their treasured little coterie. While Court had been traveling about the world and with Percy gone, Vivi had been left with the comfort of her friends. And thank heavens for them all as she had never been particularly close to either of her parents.

She winced at the notion of upsetting Charity, momentarily distracted from thoughts of the husband she hadn't expected to blow back into her life with all the turmoil of a thunderstorm. "Does she truly think Lady Featherstone is the one who started it all?"

The Marchioness of Featherstone was an acid-tongued viper who adored stirring scandal broth and was generally feared by everyone who knew her. Which was precisely why Vivi had intended to place her in the green bedchamber, which was in a far-flung wing of the manor house where she could not spy anyone engaging in the standard country house party antics. Namely, visiting bedrooms in which they did not belong.

"She said the rumors began after Lady Featherstone paid a visit to the Grosvenor Gallery," Clementine said with a sigh. "I suppose one can never tell for certain in such matters. Gossip is so very nebulous. Why *did* you invite Lady Featherstone, dearest? Knowing you, there must have been a good reason."

There had been a good reason. An excellent one, in fact.

"Because I wished to invite Lady Edith, and unfortunately, Lady Edith goes nowhere without her mother, despite the fact that she knows no one can abide the woman," Vivi explained.

"Lady Edith," Clementine repeated, her tone contemplative. "I do believe I've only chatted with her on a few occasions. A quiet young lady with great poise. Doesn't speak much, but who can blame her with that dragon of a mama? Likely, Lady Featherstone shall breathe fire on her if she says anything the slightest bit untoward."

Poor Lady Edith had indeed been saddled with an albatross. There was no denying it.

"All the more reason for her to seek like-minded friends. I thought that perhaps she might join our cause."

"Become a part of the Lady's Suffrage Society?" Clementine's brows arched. "Lady Edith? I daresay Lady Featherstone would never allow it."

"Perhaps it is time that Lady Edith stepped from under her mother's dragon wings," she suggested. "All she needs is the support of a few friends to help her fly from the nest. I feel certain of it. Besides, there will be an ample number of marriageable gentlemen in attendance. If nothing else, you can put your matchmaking skills to use on her behalf."

Clementine's blue eyes lit up at the suggestion. "You must give me a list of all the suitable men. I'm certain I could find someone for her."

Her friend was rather notorious for her matchmaking tendencies. The number of society marriages for which she was responsible continued to climb. And while Clementine remained unwed herself, Vivi knew she could not resist the chance to meddle in future courtships.

"There's the spirit," Vivi said. "We shall merely do our utmost to avoid Lady Featherstone."

"Have you an abandoned, suitably Gothic hunting lodge we can lock her away in at Sherborne Manor?" Clementine asked hopefully.

Vivi chuckled, grateful for her friend's presence and wit. Relieved to laugh. This—the sisterhood of her friends and the immense reward of a country house party that would become the talk of Society—was all she needed. Her foolish, unrequited love for Court had been extinguished by his absence. He could pack up his trunks and go back to Paris. Or better yet, some island in the middle of the sea, where he could promptly become stranded, never to dally with Parisian beauties ever again.

"I'm afraid not," she told her friend, trying not to think of her husband or the rumored antics that had crushed her heart anew when the gossip had reached her.

Curse him. He had intruded on her thoughts once again.

Just as he was intruding on her sanctuary. When she had been dressing to leave for the train station, she had heard the telltale thumps and rustles of the servants settling him in to the chamber next door. Which reminded her. She was going to have to ask one of the footmen to nail boards over the door adjoining her chamber to Court's. How to do so without causing untoward gossip? *Hmm*, she would have to think upon it.

17

Clementine sighed then. "Could we arrange for a high-wayman to run away with her *en route* from the train station?"

Vivi shook her head, another much-needed laugh torn from her at her friend's antics. "This isn't the eighteenth century, dear."

"Of course it isn't." Clementine gave her head a small, exaggerated toss that made the brunette wisps that had escaped her chignon in her travels bob. "If it were, we would all be wearing panniers and terrible wigs, and the gentlemen would go about in dreadful knee breeches and we'd be obligated to sigh over their manly calves. I cannot fathom how anyone survived that era. I once wore a wig for a masque ball, and I'll never do it again. I was sweating a river by the time the night was over, and my head itched."

"We are most fortunate," Vivi agreed. "Although I'm not certain bustles were a fair trade for the panniers."

"It is never a fair trade for women. We still don't even have the vote," Clementine grumbled.

"We are trying, however, which is what makes the work of the Lady's Suffrage Society that much more important," she asserted. "I'm a firm believer that if we are to advance our cause, we must win over the gentlemen in our lives first, and that is part of the reason I wished to hold this house party."

The other reason was far more personal. Vivi hated being alone. Because when she was alone, she thought of Court, and when she thought of Court, the tiny broken fragments of her heart that still remained ached unbearably.

"Do you think Bradford will disapprove of your involvement?" Clementine asked.

Like so many things about her, Vivi's involvement in the Lady's Suffrage Society was a development that had occurred after Court had left. He knew nothing about it. The gentleman she had once believed him to be would have been proud of her efforts on behalf of women's suffrage. But his actions had proven to her that she had never truly known him. And the austere stranger who had returned from his time abroad remained an even greater mystery to her.

"I don't care if he does," she said, and not without bitterness. "I don't give a fig about what he thinks. I am my own woman, and I have been for the last year without him. I don't need his approval. I never have."

That was what she had been telling herself repeatedly ever since she had emptied a vase of flowers on him and left him standing in the great hall, shocked and dripping. She had hastened to the privacy of her chamber, abandoning her humiliatingly damp and soiled old dress for an elegant gold silk afternoon gown far more befitting of a duchess than the rags she had been wearing. Had she only known her errant husband would make a sudden return, she certainly would have been dressed to greet him. And she would have had a horse bucket at hand to dump on him instead of something as civilized as a vase.

"Huzzah, dearest friend. The Duke of Bradford can go for a swim in the Thames with leaden weights about his ankles after the deplorable manner in which he has treated you." Clementine gave her arm a consoling pat. "Is he intending to remain for the house party, do you suppose?"

Determination made Vivi's spine go straight. "Not if I can help it."

CHAPTER 4

His wife came charging into the room in a flurry of gold silk and outraged fire. She was breathtaking in her ire, the old, sodden skirts and endearing smear of dirt on her cheek of earlier nowhere to be found. Instead, she was every inch the regal duchess who had apparently taken Society by storm during the year of his travels. She bore no resemblance to the barefoot girl who had once raced after him and Percy in the meadow at her family's country estate and who had effortlessly climbed apple trees by their sides.

"What are you doing in here?" she demanded coldly, stopping halfway across the chamber and pinning him with a glare that made her opinion of him desperately apparent.

He was no better than the horse dung in the street.

He held her gaze, thinking he had been foolish to hope he could return to her without the pain of the past interceding. Time had not erased the unpleasantness, nor could they undo what had already been done. And it was apparent that the Vivi who had begged him to stay was not the same woman as the icy goddess before him.

"I am doing what one does in a library," he told her calmly.

In truth, he was touring his ancestral home, which had changed greatly while he had been away. There had been grumbling complaints from Mother in her letters, and yet Court hadn't been prepared for the true extent of the transformation. Vivi's hand was everywhere.

"Yes, but this is *my* library," she said pointedly. "And you are not welcome in it."

"I begin to think I am not welcome anywhere within these walls," he told her, sliding the spine of the volume he had been perusing at her entrance back onto its shelf.

Even the books had been changed. The grim Latin tomes of his forebears and other achingly boring works had been removed. In their place were poetry and novels. New books with fresh spines by authors who were living contemporaneously instead of long dead. Briefly, he wondered what she had done with the old books, before deciding he didn't care.

Her full lips tightened, and she tilted her head at him in a way that was at once familiar and yet new. "Why should you believe that you were?"

"Because this is my home." The words felt strange on his tongue as he pushed away from the shelves and moved toward her. "Because you are my wife."

And that word felt odd too. She was the wife he had taken in the wake of his best friend's death, torn between the desire he felt for her and the crushing despair of losing the man who had been like a brother to him.

But she *was* his wife, even if the appellation felt unfamiliar for its lack of use. She was his wife, whom he had hurt. His sunshine-haired, freckled, beautiful girl who had been fearless and bold and wild. But she was different now. She had blossomed into an elegant duchess who looked at him with knives in her eyes and spoke to him with ice in her heart.

How could she be so familiar, and yet so much a stranger? She was at once his home and his heartbreak, his greatest comfort and his everlasting regret.

"You're too late in remembering that I am your wife," she said quietly. "And presently, the duty feels quite foreign, given your extended absence."

What could he say to that? She was right. He had made a terrible mistake in leaving her as he had, though it had taken him a great deal of time to realize that, lost in the abyss of grief and the guilt of the desire he felt for Vivi. A desire he had promised Percy he would never act on years ago before his friend's death. It was the only vow he had ever broken.

"Is that what I am to you, Vivi? A duty?" He reached for her, unable to help himself.

Needing to touch her. His heart was thundering hard in his chest despite her angry reaction to his return, despite her cool aloofness. God, how he had missed this woman in his life, in his heart, in his bed. He felt so much in that moment. Too much.

He felt everything.

But she flinched away from his hand, his fingers only succeeding in glancing over silk before she flitted to the opposite end of the library like a startled butterfly.

"I want you to leave, Court," she told him instead of answering his question, stopping before a mullioned window to gaze down at the sprawling park below. "I am expecting guests in two weeks' time, and Lady Clementine has already arrived. It would be best for you to go before anyone else comes to Sherborne Manor. The fewer witnesses to our acrimonious marriage, the less salacious gossip shall be spread. Our estrangement is already well known in Society. Your presence here will only muddy the waters unnecessarily."

The resentment in her voice was like the barbs of a thousand tiny pinpricks all at once. But one word concerned him more than all the rest.

"Our estrangement?" he repeated.

"Yes, our estrangement." She enunciated each syllable crisply, her voice carrying a whiplike crack. "How else would you characterize your abandonment of me for an entire year, Bradford?"

Was that how she saw the time he had spent away from England? That he had abandoned her?

"I didn't abandon you, Vivi. I always intended to return." Court struggled to find a means of sufficiently expressing the turbulent emotions so at odds within him.

There had been grief, vast and deep and all-consuming, upon word of Percy's drowning at sea. And then there had been the night he had surrendered to the long-burning desire for his best friend's sister and the accompanying intense guilt of betrayal that had suffocated him afterward. He had hoped that time and distance would diminish the ache, that if he repented long enough, he would be able to forgive himself.

"You intended to return," she scoffed, her lip curling in a sneer. And even looking at him as if he were the lowest creature alive laid before her, she was the most beautiful sight he had ever beheld. "What a comforting thought."

Her biting sarcasm was not lost on him.

"You didn't always have such enmity toward me," he said, trying to find the old Vivi. The Vivi he'd once known so well. The Vivi he had held in his arms the night when they had found solace in each other.

She shot him a seething glance now. "That was before you left me alone in England without a backward glance. Before I was subject to all the stories of your womanizing ways on the Continent."

He hadn't womanized. He had been faithful during his absence and his travels. He had expected she would have done the same. For the first time, he wondered if she had strayed. If she had spent time in another man's bed, in his arms. His gut clenched violently at the thought. Regardless, her assessment was unfair.

"I was not an unfaithful husband." He held her gaze. "You know why I left."

"No." She shook her head, the ice leaving her for a moment, sadness shining through the polished veneer she had donned. "I don't know why. I've never understood it, not that morning and not any of the mornings that have followed. But nor do I care any longer. The past is where it belongs. Where *you* belong. Now, if you please, see your trunks packed. There is another train leaving this afternoon, and you can easily be on it before any of my guests discover you were ever here."

He was moving again. Drawn to her, to the need to dismantle the distance she kept attempting to establish between them. Drawn to her as he had always been, from the time she had made her debut in Society and he had seen her as far more than a girl. Far more than his best friend's younger sister, though he had known he could never act upon his attraction to her.

He was suddenly furious with himself for staying away as long as he had. Furious with Percy for leaving them. Angry with Vivi for her coldness toward him, for all the ways she had changed.

For wanting her more than he ever had.

"To the devil with your guests," he returned as he joined her at the window. "I'm staying."

Her lips tightened with disapproval, but she didn't retreat this time. "What would be the point of doing so when I do not want you here?"

"I'm staying at Sherborne Manor. In your library. At your side." *In your bed*, he thought with grim, reawakened possession, but he kept the words to himself. For it was a primitive emotion, one of which he should be ashamed and wasn't sure he deserved. But the time had come. He had waited a year in deference to Percy's memory, a period of somber mourning. He had returned to claim his wife as his at last. "You cannot dismiss me like some recalcitrant servant, Vivi. I'm your husband. I belong here."

Not, perhaps, at this rambling country estate that had never felt like a true home to him. But certainly with her. They were inextricably bound.

"Why have you returned?" she snapped. "Why did you not continue to stay away? Why come now, after so long?"

"Because I am your husband, and you are my wife," he returned evenly, before uttering the words he had been practicing in his mind for the duration of the journey from New York City. "And because I have missed you."

In truth, his reasons were infinitely more. His true needs supplanted something so simplistic as words. He had been fighting against his own demons this past year, afraid of the man they made him, chased by guilt and regret. Telling her the inevitable, however, that their marriage would need to carry on despite past promises he had made, was easiest for now.

She stiffened. "Pretty words from the man who left me."

"Vivi, sweetheart." He settled his hand on her forearm gently. So gently. Fearing he would spook her, and yet needing to touch her.

But Vivi wrested her elbow from his grasp, whirling away from him, calling angrily over her shoulder as she went, "Do *not* call me your sweetheart. And do not think for one moment that I will simply fall into your bed because you have deigned to remember my existence. Everything has changed. *I've* changed. I'm no longer the foolish girl who fancied you a hero."

He stalked after her, frustrated with himself, with the decisions he had made, with the guilt that was never far, with the longing that was making his hands tremble. "I may have been gone, but I never forgot you. I thought of you every day. You never strayed from my mind. I wrote you letters whenever I had the opportunity."

She spun about, her gold silk swirling. "Letters! Do you think I wanted letters from you? Do you think I wanted a husband who ran away from me the second we were wed? Do you think I wished to be pitied and scorned whilst everyone laughed behind my back as the papers reported your exploits?"

Christ. He wondered just how bad the gossip had been. Mother had hinted at it in one of her many diatribes, but she had never explicitly detailed the reports. He would own that he had lost himself in many vices during the early weeks of his self-imposed exile. Women, however, had not been one of them.

"Vivi," he began, trying to dredge up a suitable explanation.

"No," she interrupted sharply. "You needn't try to fashion excuses for my benefit. Pray spare me the insult. I already know you didn't think about what I wanted all this time. Do you know how I know that, Bradford?" She paused, the damning silence only interrupted by the ticking of a distant antique ormolu clock. "Because you never asked me. But I am telling you now, rather than naively believing you might take it upon yourself to think of me. I want you to go, and I never want to see you again."

Her words were like a blow, knocking the air from him. And for a wild moment, he saw himself through Vivi's eyes.

She was right. He never had asked her what she wanted. He had been too consumed by his grief, guilt, and self-loathing.

"I'm sorry," he told her when he could find his voice again.

It was an apology he had owed her for a year. An apology he owed to Percy, too. Court had failed the both of them, the two people he had cared for most.

Vivi shook her head. "It's too little, too late. If you truly want my forgiveness, you'll leave me in peace."

If he were a better man, perhaps he would heed her. But he was selfish and destructive, traits that ran in the Sherborne blood. So, he reached for her instead, his hands settling on her waist as if it were where they belonged.

"I'm not leaving you again, Vivi," he said, feeling the rightness of it.

A new vow, born from the ashes of the man he'd once been. A vow he intended to keep if it was the last thing he did on earth.

And then he did what he had been dreaming of doing this interminable year they had spent apart. He lowered his head and took his wife's mouth with his.

SHOCK RENDERED Vivi immobile as Court pressed his lips to hers.

Followed immediately by sensation, almost violent in its potency. A thrilling sense of homecoming. It had been so long since he had last kissed her. Since she had watched him getting into a carriage and driving away from her.

His possessive hold on her waist seemed to sear her through layers of silk, linen, and boning. His scent wrapped around her, familiar and yet new. Clean soap with a hint of citrus and musk. The soft brush of his beard over her tender skin was foreign. Court had never, in all the years she had known him, possessed whiskers. They rendered him more masculine, less polished. Like a marauding pirate.

His mouth slanted over hers, firm and hot, and there was no denying her body's reaction—sheer jubilation. A reminder that, regardless of her anger and bitterness toward him, despite the year he had been gone, and regardless of her attempts to extinguish the feelings for him that had followed her for over a dozen years, she still loved him.

And worse, she still wanted him. Desire coiled in her belly, as dangerous as a snake because she knew the destruction he had left in his wake before. But even as she told herself she couldn't surrender, she was softening, her hands finding purchase in his coat, and she grasped his lapels, holding him tightly.

But she was at war with her body, her mind and heart struggling against each other. Somehow, she managed to hold her mouth perfectly still and refrain from returning his kiss as she so desperately longed to do. He may as well have been kissing a wall for as stubbornly as she refused to show him any hint of a reaction.

Court lifted his head, his expression impossible to discern. He looked positively barbaric, and she hated herself for the need that was pooling between her thighs, for the awareness of him that rendered his proximity an exquisite, painful temptation. She hated him and she loved him, and she wanted to kiss him and box his ears all at once.

"Kiss me, Vivi," he said, his voice low and melodious, a sensual rasp that had an effect on her all its own. "Truly kiss me and then tell me you want me to go."

She licked her lips. The gesture was foolish, indeed, because she could taste him. *Court.* And that forbidden taste made her want more.

"I'll not do it," she blurted, still clinging to him.

Reluctant to let him go.

He claimed that he intended to stay. But what did that mean? They may have married a year ago, but they had spent all the intervening time of their marriage apart. And there was the matter of those hurtful, unthinkable rumors concerning other women.

She couldn't kiss him.

She needed to kiss him.

"Do you hate me so much?" he asked softly.

Was it her imagination, or was there a hint of vulnerability in his eyes? And why should it matter if there was? One whole year, she reminded herself. There had been a time when she would have rejoiced over his arrival. When it was all she hoped for. Until so many months had passed that she had begun to believe he would simply never return.

She clung to what he had told her before he had left that awful morning.

I've made a mistake.

"I don't want you here," she repeated, for it was necessary to do so. "You made it clear before you left that you regretted marrying me. And you made it even clearer with your absence and your actions abroad."

"Vivi—" he entreated.

"No," she interrupted, furious with herself for her own weakness where he was concerned. "You cannot abandon me after telling me that you made a mistake in marrying me and then reappear in the great hall a year later, telling me that you are my husband. You cannot touch me or kiss me or look at me as you are now."

She pushed away from him, intending to flee the library and find Clementine, who had gone to her chamber with her lady's maid to unpack her trunks.

"Vivi, listen to me." He caught her elbow, halting her

flight. "I am staying for your house party whether you like it or not."

She turned back to him, knowing she could escape his grip and yet not making the effort. "I don't like it, as I have made abundantly apparent. Nor do I want it."

He released her, solemn. "You may as well accustom yourself to my presence in your life, in Sherborne Manor, at your house party. I'm not going anywhere. I'll play host to your hostess."

He was deadly serious. Although much about Court had changed, other things had not. She could hear the determination in his voice, see it in the way he held his jaw.

"You intend to humiliate me before my guests?" she demanded, her panic rising.

She had believed he would relent. That he would leave as she had asked. That she would once more have peace and the chance to recruit members to the Lady's Suffrage Society and play silly parlor games and indulge in witty conversation and distract herself by watching Clementine's matchmaking attempts.

And lawn chess.

Though that novel idea now seemed to have been hatched a lifetime ago.

"No, sweetheart," Court said quietly, almost sadly. "I intend to finally act as your husband, just as I should have done when we wed."

She ground her molars, frustration and old, stupid yearnings rising to dangerous levels within her. "Stay if you choose. But be warned, Bradford. I'll not accept your advances. I have no wish for a reconciliation. And I will never welcome you back into my bed after everything you have done."

He smiled grimly. "I've never shied from a challenge, Vivi. Not once."

She couldn't contain her reaction to his claim.

"Yes," she said bitterly, "you have."

Without another word, she turned away from him a second time and left Court alone in the library she had painstakingly assembled herself.

CHAPTER 5

*T*he next morning, following a solitary dinner the night before and an equally unaccompanied breakfast, Court found himself once more playing the part of the interloper. He had spent the better part of two hours investigating the massive, once-neglected gardens of Sherborne Manor and attempting to distract himself from Vivi's obvious attempts to avoid him. On the last occasion he had seen the gardens, they had resembled nothing so much as an overgrown thicket, complete with a silt-ridden ornamental lake and a broken fountain.

But the gardens had been restored, the lawns neatly trimmed, the rosebushes pruned and blooming. The hedge labyrinth had been sheared into tidy, box-shaped rows, and the fountain was once more tinkling merrily. Even the lake had been drained of silt and was now replete with a game of swans. So much change in just one year. He could scarcely credit it.

The late-morning sun shone down on the lake's surface, making it sparkle with a majesty that it had not possessed in all his life. It seemed, as he took a contemplative stroll on the gravel path surrounding the renewed body of water, symbolic. Vivi had always been the source of happiness and brightness in his life. Even her hair was golden and light. And now she had changed his ancestral estate as surely as she had changed him. It would seem that in his absence, in all ways, Vivi had shone.

Whilst Court...

He had been lost. Adrift on a journey of guilt and regret. Missing her.

As he rounded the lake, he approached a swan that was eyeing him dubiously from its perch on the bank. The swan opened his beak and closed it in a show of displeasure before hissing at him.

And this, too, was rather reminiscent of his present situation with his wife. Vivi was furious with him for his presence. She hadn't threatened to peck him, but she had emptied a vase upon him.

"No harm intended, old chap," he told the bird as he skirted the august creature slowly, trying to make a show of his lack of aggression.

He was just beyond the swan when he felt a sharp twinge in his left arse cheek.

The bastard had bitten him.

With a look over his shoulder to confirm the swan was flapping its wings and hissing in preparation for another strike, Court hastened his stride. Apparently, the swan was not finished with him. The bird increased his pace as well, flapping his wings and hissing, his beak opening and closing with the promise of more violence.

"Bloody hell," he muttered under his breath, changing into a run in his need to escape.

He was going to have a bruise, by God.

Court made it to a grouping of chestnut trees before he

relaxed his stride, confident he had outrun the feathered menace.

And that was when he heard it.

Feminine laughter.

But not just any laughter.

Vivi's, the sound musical and tinkling, washing over him like a caress, even if he suspected his contretemps with the swan was the source of her levity. She stood in the shade of the chestnuts, a ridiculously large-brimmed hat hiding her gorgeous blonde hair from his view, and she was wearing a navy-and-cream-striped walking gown that showed her generous bosom and well-curved waist to perfection. The moment their gazes clashed, the humor drained from her countenance. Movement at her side forced him to belatedly realize she was not alone, but rather, accompanied by a brunette dressed in a similar shade of blue, a small, jaunty hat perched atop her head. She, too, was laughing.

The Lady Clementine who had already arrived, Court supposed.

"I reckon you both witnessed my routing," he told the ladies wryly as he reached them, the cool shade of the chestnuts granting him a reprieve from the sun.

"I am afraid we did, Your Grace," his wife's friend said, still grinning at his expense. "I must say, I've never seen a swan so thoroughly irate before. Do you always have that effect on birds?"

He grimaced, sketching a bow as he did so, remembering the manners he'd been eschewing for most of the last year. "Thankfully, no."

"I do believe Honoré quite thoroughly trounced you, Your Grace," Vivi told him coolly, having schooled her features into a mask of civility.

And not without a note of pride, he thought, rather as if she had pinned her hopes on the odds of his walking past the angry cob at just the right moment for the attack. If he hadn't known better, he would have sworn she had planned the entire affair.

"Tell me you haven't named that wretched beast Honoré," he said, though he wasn't surprised that she had.

For Vivi had always named every creature she came upon. There had been Frederick the Frog, Charles the stables cat, Alberta the hunting hound, and a host of others over the years. He found himself smiling at the discovery of a part of her which had not changed in his absence.

"There is nothing wrong with his name," Vivi informed him.

"A bit grandiose for a feathered nuisance," he grumbled, resisting the urge to rub his smarting arse.

He had no doubt he would have a bruise there. Deserved, it was true.

"You don't like him because he bit you," she countered.

"Seems sufficient reason, does it not?" He turned his attention to the brunette at her side, whom she had yet to introduce. "Lady Clementine, I presume?"

She inclined her head. "I fear my reputation precedes me."

Reputation? He sent a look in Vivi's direction, wondering what manner of people she had surrounded herself whilst he had been gone. Mother's letters had always been sharply worded and filled with implications he hadn't wished to consider. *The duchess travels in a fast set*, she had written once, before droning on for five paragraphs about the forward and wrongheaded nature of the suffragists, artists, and writers Vivi had befriended in London, many of whom had apparently visited Sherborne Manor with her. He wondered again whether she had been faithful to him, but then he tamped down the unwanted thoughts.

"As a matchmaker," Vivi explained with a frown.

He clasped his hands behind his back, feeling foolish after

the nonsense with Honoré the bloodthirsty swan. "Of course. Is that the nature of this house party, then? You and Vivi are playing at Cupid for your friends and acquaintances?"

He directed his question to Lady Clementine, whose demeanor possessed significantly less ice and condemnation than his wife's.

"Perhaps," Lady Clementine answered vaguely, casting a searching look in Vivi's direction that spoke volumes and only served to heighten his curiosity.

Why was this blasted house party so important to Vivi? And what secrets were the two ladies before him keeping?

"Or perhaps not," he guessed, swinging his gaze back to Vivi, who had been studying him intently.

Pink blossomed on her cheeks, and he wondered at the cause of it. What had she been thinking? Had it been about him? He hoped so. Their parting the day before in the library had been unpleasant, but he remained determined to win her back however he must. Still, she could not avoid him forever, and this little reunion was proof of that.

"If you must know, my guests are either members of the Lady's Suffrage Society or future members we are interested in inviting to join our cause," she said loftily.

Mother had not been wrong about that detail, then. But unlike her, Court did not have any concern about Vivi's involvement in the Lady's Suffrage Society. He believed that women should gain the right to vote. Some of Mother's beliefs harkened to a previous century, but there was no altering her opinion. He'd never met someone less inclined to see reason.

"You are a member yourself, then," he said to Vivi, admiring her loveliness.

It felt as if a lifetime had passed since their parting the day before. She was all cool, icy poise this morning, not a golden curl out of place, her rose-petal-pink lips pinched at the corners with disapproval for him. He longed to undo her buttons, to toss away her hat to reveal the full glory of her hair. To kiss her until she was breathless and make her forget all the hurt in her heart. Not going to her last night as he had wanted had been sheer agony, but he had promised himself he would grant her the time she needed to accustom herself to his renewed presence in her life.

Her chin went up, defiance flashing in her blue eyes. "If I am?"

She had never been so defensive and guarded with him before. She had always been open and teasing and earnest. He hated her aloofness, her lack of trust, and loathed even more that he was the cause of it. Her refusal to respond to his kiss still stung. She had kissed him with fierce passion once, as if she had drawn her very life from his mouth on hers, and he fully intended to have those kisses again one day.

"Then I commend you," he told her softly. "It is a worthy cause."

"I shall leave you and His Grace to talk," Lady Clementine said, reminding Court of her hovering presence.

He had quite forgotten, so caught up was he in Vivi.

Court cleared his throat, feeling oddly as if he had been caught in a state of dishabille, for his emotions were that raw and near to the surface. He hadn't felt so gauche since he'd been a green young buck of sixteen, experiencing his first kiss.

"That isn't necessary," Vivi blurted.

"It was a pleasure meeting you, Lady Clementine," he said in the same moment.

The lady in question looked from him to Vivi, catching her lower lip in her teeth as she no doubt debated which of them she should listen to.

"Bradford can carry on his way," Vivi added, shooting him a glare. "Clementine and I were just discussing the final details concerning our life-size game of lawn chess. Weren't we, dear?" She directed the last question to her friend, smiling brightly.

"Was that why there were painters on the north lawn?" he asked, comprehension dawning.

He'd been too consumed by his whirling thoughts to travel the distance to question the fellow, contented to watch the bustling activity from afar instead. For in that moment, lingering in the newly rejuvenated roses had been like being close to her, and he needed that nearness. Even if the woman before him was every bit as thorny as the flowers.

"I do hope you didn't intervene." Vivi frowned. "Shipley knows precisely what he must do."

"Shipley?" He unclasped his hands, lifting one to pass over his beard, contemplating. "The name isn't familiar."

"He is the head gardener," she informed him.

That didn't sound right.

Court scratched idly at his beard. "I thought that his name was Philips."

Her lips pinched before she answered crisply. "Did you not receive word from Sterling in your travels? Shipley is the head gardener now. I'm afraid that Philips died."

Just like Percy had. The knowledge lay between them, heavy and unspoken. Percy's death was what had brought them together, but it was also what had torn them apart.

"Truly, a peaceful walk would be wonderfully restorative after the bustle of the train yesterday," Lady Clementine interrupted the silence. "I will see you both this afternoon, I hope."

With that, she scurried away down the path, in the direction of Honoré.

"Do take care when approaching the fiendish swan," he called after her. "He likes to bite."

"Forewarned is forearmed," Lady Clementine called over her shoulder with a little wiggle of her fingers.

Vivi sighed heavily, gaze trained on her friend's retreat. "I hope Honoré bit you as hard as he could."

~

Vivi watched dejectedly as her dear friend's elegant form disappeared around a bend in the lake just beyond Honoré, swallowed up by lush green foliage. So much for loyalty and sisterhood, she thought grimly. Clementine would certainly hear from her later.

For now, she was once again where she decidedly did not want to be.

Alone with Court.

Court, who was even more handsome in his country tweed than he had been yesterday in his more formal clothes.

"That is hardly wifely of you, Vivi," he said, his tone one of mock chastisement.

Once, his teasing would have been welcomed. She would have teased him in return. They would have laughed together. But there was the gaping hole of the last year between them, and she was no longer the woman she had been when he had left her, nor was he the same man she had for so long adored.

"I don't feel like a wife," she told him, reluctantly turning her attention back to him.

He was still idly stroking his neatly trimmed beard. The very whiskers that had lightly abraded her skin when he had kissed her in the library. She had liked it. And worse, she longed for his mouth on hers again, despite everything he had done. Sleeping in her chamber with him one door away had been a terrible temptation, for part of her had wanted quite desperately to bridge the distance and go to him. Her pride and the broken heart she had so diligently been trying to repair had prevented her, however.

"I could make you feel like a wife again," he suggested, his voice low and laden with sensual implication.

Again. She did not miss that lone word. She could not deny that once, he had made her feel every inch his wife. He had shown her passion she hadn't known possible. Had made her body his in every way, drowning her in pleasure.

But she wouldn't think of that now.

She swallowed hard against a rush of longing. "If you're implying you will share my bed, think again. For I'll not welcome you there."

All the teasing fled his countenance, and his eyes burned into hers with remembered desire. "We haven't always needed a bed, have we, Vivi?"

She inhaled harshly, shocked that he would dredge up such a memory now, when he had only just returned the day before and she was feeling so very raw.

"I don't know what you're speaking of," she lied just to spite him, twisting her fingers in her skirts in her agitation.

But Court did not relent. Nor did he give her the space she so desperately needed. Instead, he came closer, until her gown brushed his trousers. Until the wide brim of her picture hat nearly collided with his chin.

He canted his head, dipping it so that their faces were even. "You remember the boathouse, do you not?"

The boathouse.

Her eyes slid closed as memories washed over her.

How could she have forgotten that night, when she had shattered in his arms on the coat he had laid over the old planked floor? Court had come to Edmonds House for Percy's funeral, which had been held after futile weeks of hoping his earthly remains would wash ashore following the sinking of the *Marguerite*.

She and Court had met in the boathouse after everyone else had been long abed, just as they had with Percy so many times before. She had been weeping, and he had taken her in his arms to comfort her. But somehow, the mingled tears and comfort and pain had turned into kisses, and then those kisses had become something more.

And then eager hands had begun sweeping clothing away.

"You recall it, don't you?" Court asked quietly. "What happened between us."

Of course she did. He had made love to her that night, and they had fallen asleep tangled together, draping their discarded garments over each other, too exhausted to return to the main house. Her irate father had been the one to discover them the next morning, and marriage had been their sole recourse.

A marriage he had not wanted, a fact which Court had made more than apparent when he had left her.

"I don't want to speak of it," she told him. "It's in the past where it belongs."

"It is hardly in the past. I've thought of nothing but that night." He reached for her, his hand cupping her cheek. "That night has haunted me. Followed me across oceans and continents, until finally, I could stay away no longer, and it brought me back to you."

His hand was warm and large, his thumb stroking her cheekbone, his gaze holding hers in its relentless thrall. "You'll have to resign yourself to the fact that I intend to assert my husbandly rights at some point, Vivi."

Despite herself, his words sent wicked heat cascading over her. Her body swayed, as if she were a plant seeking the sun, because that was what Court had always been to her: heat, vitality, life. But no, she would not give in with such ease.

"When will you seek to do so?" she asked. "Here? Perhaps

against the trunk of this chestnut tree would suffice. I'll lift my skirts, and you can rut away."

Her words were ugly, and she knew it. He had never treated her with anything other than gentleness and tender care. But that had been before he had left her.

He clenched his jaw, the thumb that had been caressing her stilling. "Is that what you think of me, Vivi? That I am no better than an animal? Because if it is, let me reassure you." At this, he pulled the hat from his head and leaned nearer, his lips almost grazing hers as he spoke. "I mean to woo you. To court you. To seduce you. To do everything I should have done a year ago."

Those were words she would have longed for not long ago. Words she would have held in her heart when he had left her until the day he had abruptly returned. But the days had turned into months, and the months into a year, and her hurt and anguish had only compounded.

"Why did you not do it then, instead of leaving me?" she demanded, refusing to touch him in return, regardless of how much she yearned to do so.

"Because I wasn't ready," he murmured, his handsome face close, so close, his scent taunting her. "I wasn't worthy of you then. I hated myself for what I had done, for the promise I had broken to Percy."

Her brother's name sent a shock through Vivi. It was the first Court had spoken the name aloud, the first she had heard anyone speak it in nearly a year. She still missed her beloved brother with an aching grief from which she knew she would never fully recover. His death had been such a shock. Percy had always been brimming with life, and though he had found himself in many scrapes over the years, he had always extricated himself with aplomb. The sunken yacht, however, had taken him to a watery grave.

42

"What promise did you make my brother?" She searched Court's eyes, seeking answers. Seeking the truth.

He pressed his forehead to hers, and for a moment, they were sheltered together beneath the large, accommodating brim of her picture hat and it felt as if it was the two of them united against the world, just as it always should have been.

But then he spoke, shattering the illusion. "I promised Percy that I would never touch you."

And suddenly the reason for his yearlong absence became abundantly, terribly clear.

She drew back enough so that she could see Court's face, hold his gaze. "When?"

Vivi wasn't even certain why the timing mattered to her, and yet somehow, it did.

"Since you were eighteen and I danced with you at a ball. It was a promise I kept for years in deference to our friendship. And then, in a moment of weakness, I broke that promise, and I couldn't forgive myself for it."

She felt as if someone had knocked the air from her, and she almost doubled over to catch her breath. Vivi recalled that ball. It had been the first time Court had looked at her as if she was a woman rather than his best friend's sister. And when he had whirled her about the ballroom, hope had risen, firm and determined, in her heart. Later, when he had teased her about mud puddles and frogs at their next meeting as if she were still a girl, and he had told her she was the younger sister he had never had, she had been thrust into despair, thinking she had imagined his interest.

She was reeling, struggling to comprehend the implications of this revelation. "Percy asked you to stay away from me?"

"He was damned protective over you, just as a brother ought to be," Court said, withdrawing his hand and leaving her bereft. "He told me I was far too much of a wild rake, and back then, I cannot lie, Vivi. I was, while you were young and innocent. He feared that a dalliance between the two of us would only end in heartache for you and the ruination of my friendship with him. He was afraid I would hurt you, and he was not wrong in that. It would seem that I have, and badly."

He had turned her unrequited love to ash, but that was another matter. She was still stuck on the unsettling revelation that Court had not left because of Vivi herself, but because of some vow she had never known had been made. A vow to her brother.

Vivi shook her head, feeling as if the world had suddenly turned itself inside out. "Why would he make you promise?"

Court's expression shifted, hardening. "Because I had asked his permission to court you. He was angry. Shocked, I reckon. He had always believed I considered you a sister until that moment. He refused to hear it, and he made me swear to him that I would never touch you."

"You wanted to court me," she repeated numbly. "After the ball where we danced."

How young they had both been then, eight years ago, Court two-and-twenty to her eighteen. For one dazzling night, she had believed he could be hers. Until he had dashed her hopes, and the years had worn on while she watched him dally and flirt with others, forever beyond her reach.

One night in the wake of Percy's death had changed all that.

Court nodded grimly. "I did. But my loyalty was to Percy rather than my own desires. I vowed to him that I would leave you alone, Vivi, and then I broke that vow and I hated myself. But I also wanted you more than I ever had."

Sadness swept over her. For herself, for Court. For Percy. Sadness and understanding.

"And that is the sole reason you left me?" she prodded, needing to be certain. "Your broken promise to Percy?"

"My broken promise and the guilt and the anguish over his death. But also the fear that I wasn't worthy of you. That Percy had been right to warn me away from you. A better man would not have taken the innocence of his best friend's sister on the night of his bloody funeral."

Tears stung her eyes, blurring her vision. "Why did you not tell me all this before you left? And if not then, why not at any time? Why wait an entire year to return to me and tell me now?"

Now when it felt as if it was far too late.

"Perhaps I should have done so. I was a ruin after Percy's death. I didn't know what to do. All I knew was that I had broken my vow and betrayed him. I needed time." There was no denying the sorrow in his voice, in his eyes.

"And I needed *you*," she told him, feeling every bit as broken now as she had on the day he had driven away from her in his carriage. "But you left me. You left me for a year, with no explanation, no hope of your return, no reason you had gone. You told me our marriage was a mistake."

Her voice hitched on the last word, and she hated herself for the vulnerability. For showing just how deeply he had cut her. For showing him just how much she still cared, even when she should not.

"I'm sorry," he told her, regret lacing his voice. "Sorrier than you'll ever know."

"It's not enough." She blinked hard to keep the tears from falling. "Now, I am the one who needs time and distance."

With that grim pronouncement, she moved away from him, needing to flee for the second time in as many days.

"Vivi," he called after her.

But her feet kept going, taking her down the path that led away from the manor house and everything and everyone who could hurt her.

CHAPTER 6

"*Y*our Grace," Lady Clementine said, surprise coloring her voice. "I thought you were speaking with Vivi."

He had caught up to his wife's friend after Vivi had left him standing alone in the chestnut grove. They were well beyond the ill-tempered swan, approaching the rose garden.

"I was *trying* to speak with her," he acknowledged wryly. "However, I fear I upset her instead."

Court didn't blame Vivi for her reaction, of course. But he wished she had not run from him, even if he understood her reason and respected her need for solitude. The house party was beginning in a fortnight, and he was running out of time to have his wife all to himself. He couldn't shake the fear that when she was surrounded by her guests, it would be easier for her to put distance between them. Easier for her to avoid him. Easier for her to cling to her hurt and anger and refuse to give him a second chance.

"Oh dear," Lady Clementine murmured, her countenance turning fraught. "Where is she now? Shall I go and find her?"

"I'm sure she would appreciate your company," he said, "but I was hoping I might have a conversation with you first."

Her brows rose. "With me, Your Grace?"

"Please, call me Bradford," he invited, disliking the formality intensely as he always had, "or better yet, Court, as all my friends do."

She eyed him warily, her expression turning pensive. "I'm not certain it would be wise for me to be your friend, given the circumstances."

He gusted out a heavy sigh. "I'll not argue the point. But since you are a friend of my wife's, you are a friend of mine."

"Given the way you've treated her this last year, you are more likely my enemy," Lady Clementine said tartly.

And he didn't blame her for the opinion.

"I appreciate your loyalty to Vivi," he said, meaning those words wholeheartedly. "I'm hoping it is that same loyalty which will allow you to give me some advice concerning my present circumstances."

In the past, when he had needed to consult anyone about the women in his life, it had always been Percy. He couldn't deny that asking someone else for aid felt wrong. He missed his friend. Missed their easy camaraderie. Missed everything about him.

"I'll try," Lady Clementine conceded, and he took note for the first time that her hat was bedecked with a clump of silk roses that looked remarkably similar to the blooms in which they stood, bees buzzing happily around them.

"Thank you." He paused, frowning as a bee chose that moment to fly toward the decoration on her hat. "Hold still, Lady Clementine."

Her eyes went wide. "What is it?"

"Nothing more than a bee." He doffed his hat, using its brim to chase the trespasser. "There you are. I didn't want it to sting you."

"Disaster averted." She gave him a small smile, and he wondered if perhaps his act of gallantry had slightly improved her estimation of him. "I suppose you're not as hideously evil as I had previously supposed."

Well, then.

He settled his hat atop his head with a sardonic smile. "How reassuring. Shall we walk as we talk, Lady Clementine? I have a suspicion that if we linger, we'll only invite more such incidents."

She nodded. "I suppose we should. What is it you wished to discuss with me?"

They began a slow promenade to the main house, passing through the roses toward the fountain.

"I have a plan," he began, "and I'm wondering if you might be willing to aid me in it..."

VIVI REINED in Visigoth when she reached the outskirts of the old castle wall. Lynwood Castle was one of the original settlements at Sherborne Manor, dating to the fourteenth century, but it had been left abandoned in favor of the manor house some time in the eighteenth century by a past Duke of Bradford. During the weekend house parties she had been holding this summer, it had become a favorite haunt for all her guests. She'd had the interior inspected for damage, the first level swept and cleared, and the old stables repaired enough for use.

When Clementine had sent her a note that afternoon suggesting they meet at the castle for a picnic dinner, Vivi had leapt at the chance. She knew Court would never find them here, for the castle was sufficiently far from the main house. The opportunity to continue eluding him was too tempting to resist. She was still badly shaken from his morning revelations, and after leaving him by the lake, she had diverted her attention to all tasks related to the house party and the impending arrival of her guests in two weeks' time.

Any time she had spied him, she had thrown herself into a conversation with a nearby domestic, thwarting his attempts to speak to her. Which reminded her, she thought grimly as she dismounted from Visigoth, she still needed to decide which footman she could entrust with the task of hammering wooden slats over the door connecting her bedroom to Court's. It would be best to have it done before her guests descended upon Sherborne Manor. Fewer opportunities for anyone to hear the noise, ask questions, and carry tales.

It was bad enough that she would have to suffer the pretense of a happy marriage with Court for the sake of her guests and her pride. No need to add further duress. Carefully, Vivi led her mount to the stables and secured him within before venturing into the inner bailey of the castle.

But what she saw there made her stop.

For it wasn't her friend Clementine awaiting her on a large blanket that had been spread over the ground, a picnic hamper at his side. Instead, it was Court.

"You," she said.

"Me." He rose to his feet with effortless masculine grace, offering her an elegant bow. "Good evening, wife."

Wife.

He had used the title before, but there was something different about it now, within the walls of Lynwood. It rolled off his tongue like an endearment. She couldn't quell the sudden surge of longing that rose within her.

"What are you doing here?" she demanded, feeling almost as if they were in a farce together in which he unrepentantly appeared when she least expected him. Three times in a row now, he had surprised her with his presence. "Where is Clementine?"

"Lady Clementine is dining back at the house," he said easily, striding forward with supreme confidence.

A confidence she couldn't help but admire. He had always walked that way, as if all the world were at his mercy. She certainly had been from the moment she had first seen him.

Vivi forced herself to think of her dear friend, who had apparently betrayed her. But no, surely Clementine would not take up Court's cause. She and Clementine had been inseparable since they had met at a gathering held by Lady Josephine Decker in London some months ago.

"Why is she at the house?" Vivi asked, suspicion rising. "Did you discover our plans and seek to ruin them?"

"Of course not." He stopped before her, offering her his arm just as gallantly as he had on that ballroom floor eight years ago. "I enlisted her aid, and given that I saved her from a bee that was intent on making its home in her hat, she was willing to agree."

The mentioning of the bee momentarily distracted her. "It is all the flowers she wears, always dripping from her hats and gowns. But if I didn't know better, I would swear that you somehow cozened that bee into abetting you."

A half grin kicked up one corner of his mouth. "Buzz."

His droll reaction startled a laugh from her. The moment it emerged, she clapped her hand over her lips, irritated with herself for succumbing to his easy charm.

"You may laugh at me, Vivi. Better yet, laugh *with* me." He raised his elbow incrementally, as if to remind her he was awaiting her response. "Now, take my arm and allow me to escort you to dinner."

She eyed his arm, trying not to allow herself to succumb to all the emotions fluttering inside her. Here was, at once, the Court she remembered so well. Magnetic, witty, handsome. And inside, she was melting for him just as she always had. Desperate for the smiles she had watched him bestow upon others for so many years until he had finally been hers.

Until the very next day, when he hadn't been.

"You tricked me," she said.

And you hurt me, she added in her mind. *You broke my heart and left me without a backward glance.*

"Tell me honestly." He tilted his head in considering fashion, pinning her with a knowing stare. "Would you have joined me if you had known the invitation was from me instead of Lady Clementine?"

"Of course not," she admitted without hesitation.

His lips firmed, the only hint that her words had displeased him. "I've only a fortnight to have you to myself before your guests arrive. Do you blame me for wanting to make the best of it?"

"For deceiving me and for somehow persuading my dearest friend to abet your lies?" she asked tartly, not about to relent. "Is that your definition of making the best of the evening?"

Her stomach was hungry, and it was a longish ride back to the manor house. The picnic spread out behind him looked terribly inviting, the walls of Lynwood enclosing them in an almost magical realm out of time. But she would not forget the reason for all her anger toward him. Nor all the pain she had endured the last year, believing he had left her because he did not want her. No. Indeed, he was going to have to work for her acquiescence.

The expression on his face shifted, and there was no denying the blatant sensual intent. He was positively smoldering with it.

"Do you truly wish to know my definition of making the best of the evening with you, Vivi?" he asked with deceptive softness.

51

The air between them changed, sparking hot with awareness despite the coolness of the old stone walls surrounding them and the trees beyond blotting out what remained of the evening sun. She should tell him no, she knew. And yet, part of her—the old, long-buried part of her that had loved him from afar for so many years—desperately wanted to hear whatever he had to say.

Dear God.

The reason hit her then with sudden, awful clarity.

She had never stopped loving him. And how could she, when loving Court had been a part of her for the last twelve years, since she had been fourteen?

The ability to speak fled her, choked by pent-up emotion.

"I've never seen you at a loss for words before." He frowned, lowering his arm. "Have I made you hate me so much that you won't even deign to join me for dinner?"

"Tell me," she blurted, hating herself for surrendering to the need, tears of shame and longing burning in her eyes. "What is your definition of making the best of the evening with me?"

He held her stare, his countenance solemn, the roguish flirt who had greeted her nowhere to be found now. Instead, he was simply himself—or rather, this new version. This bearded, serious, vexingly masculine, irritatingly determined Court.

"First, I would kiss you," he said, proving that he could make her want him without so much as a touch. "I would kiss you until you melted into me and kissed me back. And then I would take your hand in mine and lead you to the picnic. I'd unpack the apple pudding and tell you to take a bite of that first."

Vivi adored apple pudding. She had for as long as she could recall.

"You remember," she said, trying her utmost not to think about the first portion of his statement.

The kissing bit.

"That it is one of your favorites?" He smiled, and it was a rare, beautiful smile. "How could I forget? You always fed half your dinners to Alberta, but the apple pudding never made it to the hound. Not even once."

Dear, sweet Alberta. As Percy's favorite, the hound had been as much of a fixture in their home as the gas lamps on the wall. They had mourned her passing as if she were another sibling. For she had been, albeit a furred one.

A new wave of sadness hit Vivi. "She was a lovely dog. She was inordinately fond of bacon."

"And all manner of cheese," Court said.

She wanted to hate him, but she loved him. Wanted to push him away, but he had remembered Alberta. He had recalled her own love of apple pudding.

"You have apple pudding in the hamper?" she asked him, slanting a curious glance in the direction of the picnic he had laid out.

He smiled again. "Would I arrange for a picnic with my Vivi and forget the apple pudding?"

She was about to tell him that she was decidedly not *his* Vivi when he took her hand in his and guided it to the crook of his elbow.

"Never," he added.

And then he led her to the blanket he had spread in the bailey of Lynwood, and she decided that perhaps there wasn't any harm in sharing apple pudding with Court after all.

CHAPTER 7

"*J*ust one more bite of the apple pudding," Court urged Vivi as they sat at a proper distance opposite each other on the counterpane. "Look at how much remains. It's a sin to waste Cook's delicacies."

"I couldn't." She shook her head, resting her hand lightly on her stomach. "You brought enough food to feed an entire infantry brigade."

She exaggerated, but perhaps he had requested too much sustenance be packed in the hamper for just the two of them. As it stood, his primary hunger was for Vivi herself, and no amount of cold ham, cheeses, roast chicken, or apple pudding would sate him. It had required all the restraint he possessed to remain where he was as they shared their repast instead of crawling across the blanket and devouring her as he longed to do. But he knew she needed time and wooing, and he intended to give her everything she required and more.

"I hope you enjoyed the picnic, despite the company you were forced to keep," he said lightly, bracing himself on one flattened palm as he crossed his ankles in an effort to keep his thundering need for her at bay.

Her spine stiffened, and he regretted his words, the reminder that they were at daggers drawn. Perhaps she had forgotten during their easy meal, when they had been more concerned with the food and wine laid before them than the past and the ugly shadow it cast on the present.

"I enjoyed it well enough," she said primly, reaching for her wineglass and bringing it to her lips.

Her grudging response was perhaps a small victory.

He took a sip of his own wine, considering his next words with care. "You said there was gossip about me whilst I was abroad. Might I ask what was said?"

"I would prefer not to discuss it." Her voice was quiet, laced with hurt.

"I fear we must," he told her gently. "I cannot speak to the scandal broth unless I know what it is."

She huffed a small sigh, her sky-blue gaze flitting away from his, settling on the remnants of her apple pudding. "It was said that you were an honored guest of the Baroness d'Olivier in Paris. And that you attended one of Lady Hazle-hurst's grand parties."

He hadn't known his actions were fodder for so much gossip. If he had, he would have taken greater care. His every interaction had been innocent enough, however, and was easily explained.

"The Baroness is fifteen years my senior and a friend of my mother's," he said. "She insisted I join her for a dinner one evening while I was in Paris, and I accepted out of obligation."

"Her reputation precedes her," Vivi grumbled, frowning at him as she swung her gaze back to his. "Surely you are aware of that."

The baroness did indeed have a well-known appetite for lovers. As far as Court could tell, she and the baron were happy to live their lives separately and to share their beds with whomever they liked.

"I understand that she and her husband enjoy a certain arrangement," he said judiciously. "However, I can assure you that there is only one woman whose bed I wish to share, and she is most assuredly not the Baroness d'Olivier."

"And what of Lady Hazlehurst, then?" she asked next, clearly ignoring the implication in his words. "Surely she is not also a friend of the dowager's."

The widowed Marchioness of Hazlehurst was a collector of paintings and *objets d'art*. She was also a vivacious flirt and a Parisian hostess famed for her wild fêtes and string of lovers. But she'd been in possession of something Court had desperately wanted—a singing bird box just like the one Percy had given to Vivi years before, only for it to have been lost in a small library fire at Edmonds House. He had the bird box packed in a trunk that would hopefully be arriving soon; sending it to her had felt somehow wrong, and carrying it with him during his travels had felt like keeping a part of her near to him.

"She had something of great personal value to me in her possession," he answered honestly. "I attended her gathering with the intent of speaking to her about it, nothing more."

"And what was it that she had in her possession?" Vivi demanded to know, her voice taking on a note of suspicion, as if she didn't believe him and was intent upon finding a hole in his explanation.

"I can't tell you now."

Her brows drew together. "Why not?"

"Because it would spoil the surprise, sweetheart."

Her silk skirts were artfully arranged about her, cleverly

hiding everything but her embroidered boots from view. He was sorely tempted to trail his fingers over a boot, to trace the cream-colored flowers and intricate emerald vines, skim beyond the laces, and find her calf.

"Don't call me that, if you please," she said tartly, fidgeting with her skirt as if she could sense the war raging within him.

"Sweetheart?" He gave her a look. "I thought it was only *dear* that caused you to dump vases over me. Fortunately, there are no filled vases within sight."

Court was daring to tease her again. For all the years he had known her, since she'd been but a girl—Percy's intrepid little sister who nattered on about birds and poetry and butterflies and dogged their every step—his relationship with Vivi had been easy. They had been friends first. And later, when she had grown into a woman, his feelings for her had altered, and he had seen her as so much more than the girl who had gamely raced him across the fields and who had once hidden a frog in his left boot. He longed for the same easiness between them, for the ice to begin thawing.

"You deserved far more than a dumped vase for leaving me this past year," Vivi told him solemnly.

Very likely, he did. He wouldn't argue the point, for it would serve neither of them. He had already explained to her why he had left. Why he had stayed away. Vivi would have to choose whether she could forgive him. Whether she chose to give him a second chance to set their marriage to rights.

"A frog in my boot, perhaps," he suggested, striving to keep their conversation from descending into heavier subjects.

He wanted to remind her—to remind them both—of how it had been between them before. Of how it could be between them again. An easy camaraderie. Husband and wife. Lovers. One thing had become abundantly clear to him in his absence, and it was that he wanted a future with Vivi. He wanted happiness, laughter, lovemaking. One day, he hoped, children.

"I tried that tactic once before," she said, plucking at her skirts in a gesture he instantly recognized.

She was conflicted.

"And you feared I would step on the frog and smash him when I put on my boots," he reminisced. "So you slipped back into my chamber and laid the boot on its side."

"But then, the frog hopped under your bed and kept you up all night with his croaking," she finished, smiling at him.

God, her smile took his breath. Took him back in time to that pivotal moment when he had watched her whirling beneath the chandeliers with another man at the Marquess of Needham's ball. The golden glints in her hair had shone, and she had been wearing a silk gown that matched. The need to dance with her had consumed him.

And when he'd taken her in his arms, the need for Vivi had supplanted all else. It had never ceased, even if he had struggled to keep his distance in deference to Percy.

He chuckled softly as he forced himself to think of the frog instead of the interceding time that was forever lost to them both. "By morning light, I was about to rout the little beggar and force him from under the bed, but not without a dreadful night's sleep. When I returned him to you, you told me quite sternly that his name was Frederick the Frog and not This Pernicious Creature, as I had been referring to him."

"It was hardly Frederick's fault that you gave him such a fright," Vivi said. "I expect he was quite terrified of you bellowing at him all night. You were terribly Friday faced when you came to breakfast that morning. Even Percy said that he would hide from you if he were me, for fear of the retaliation."

"You would have been as well, had you been forced to listen to Frederick the Frog's nonsense all night long," he drawled.

They smiled at each other, lost in the silliness of the past. Fond memories. All the ties, so inextricable, that bound them together.

Desperation and desire seized him then, and he surrendered to the need to move closer to her, hauling himself across the counterpane with a complete and utter lack of grace and not giving a damn. He didn't stop until he was at her side, sweeping plates and serviettes and serving trays aside to make room for himself. Court reached for her, cupping her cheek, running his thumb slowly over her sleek, soft skin.

"Wh-what are you doing?" she stammered, but she made no move to extricate herself or push him away.

Her eyes were wide, still pools of endless blue, and he wanted to drown in them. "God, I've missed you, Vivi," he confessed, instead of answering her question, for it was apparent what he was doing.

He was touching her.

Touching her as he had yearned to do all their time apart.

He lowered his head, his mouth seeking hers.

And kissing her. For the simple reason that he would perish from wanting her if he did not.

COURT'S LIPS were on hers, hot and firm and right, so very right.

The last time he had kissed her, she hadn't responded.

But this time, she had no choice. Vivi had lost control and all sense of pride. Because Court was being his old, sweet, teasing self, and because he was dredging up dear memories of how everything between them once was, and because she was feeling desperately raw after his sudden return and revelations. She reached for him, her hand finding purchase on his broad, muscular shoulder while holding herself upright with the other, her palm flattened on the blanket, the coolness of the bailey ground seeping through. And she kissed him back.

Opened for him, sighing into his mouth as his tongue slid inside hers. He groaned, gliding his fingers from her cheek to the back of her head, cupping her nape in a possessive hold that would have made her knees knock together had she been standing. Instead, liquid desire pooled between her thighs.

He had missed her?

She had missed him more.

Vivi kissed him harder. The frenzied rush of longing inside her was the same as it had been in the boathouse, only stronger, fortified by a year of yearning and the memory of how masterfully he had made love to her. She wasn't certain if she could forgive him yet. Not so easily, nor so quickly. But she did know that her body needed his in an elemental sense.

He broke the kiss to drag his mouth along her jaw, stringing a line of kisses to her ear. "Ah, Vivi. Sweet Vivi. Will you allow me to make amends?"

She didn't know what his whispered question meant, but his breath was a warm distraction making more desire unfurl inside her, and she was suddenly beyond the ability to concentrate or make sense of anything other than his lips.

His lips and his teeth, which caught her earlobe and tugged. His tongue, too, as he licked that secret hollow behind her ear that drove her to distraction. He'd found it that night in the boathouse, and it made her melt.

She had forgotten, but bittersweet remembrance hit her

now. Remembrance of just how inevitable it had felt that night when he had stripped away her gown and chemise. When his head had dipped and he had taken one of her nipples in his mouth, and the most exquisite burst of fiery pleasure had taken her by surprise. It had been nothing compared to when he had parted her folds and found the insistent bud hidden within.

Pleasure coiled inside her as he reverently traced his lips along her throat. She allowed her head to fall back so that he could rake his beard along the sensitive skin, the abrasion making a needy sigh leave her. She clawed at his lapel, wanting the coat off his shoulder. Wanting fewer layers keeping her from his skin. Wanting him and furious with him and so in love with him that it hurt.

"Your answer, Vivi," he prodded, his teeth grazing the cord of her neck. "Will you?"

The answer for Court was *yes*. It always had been. It forever would be yes. He was hers, the man who owned her heart. Her husband, her lover, her everything.

But part of her was coherent enough to sternly cling to her pride.

"You may try," she said, succeeding in guiding his coat off his shoulder.

He shrugged the tweed away, the garment falling limply to the counterpane, and then she had a shirt and a waistcoat keeping her from what she wanted. He lifted his head, holding her stare, the passion burning hot in his eyes undeniable.

"I'll try my damnedest," he promised. "I'll never stop. I want to be a good husband to you, Vivi. The husband you deserve."

She wasn't ready to hear these long-wished-for vows from him just yet. She wanted to feel instead of think. To allow herself to get swept away here with no one else about and the centuries-old ruins of Lynwood Castle towering above them. She wanted what she had been missing these long twelve months without him.

And to prove to herself that she was so very different from the wife who had watched him drive away in his carriage—to prove it to Court as well—she kissed him. Pressed her mouth to his with such aggression that her inner lip cut into her teeth. But she didn't care. She was taking what she wanted this time.

He issued a guttural groan of pure longing, and she loved it. Loved the hint that he was not nearly as polished and calm as he pretended. That under his signature sangfroid and easy teasing lay a man who burned for her every bit as much as she burned for him. Boldly, she slipped her tongue into his mouth, and he sucked on it. Her nipples were hard, aching points behind the shield of her corset, and her body clamored for his touch, for his possession.

Suddenly, the kiss was no longer sufficient. She wanted, needed, *had* to have more. She tore her lips from his and gathered fistfuls of her cumbersome skirts, hefting them up so that she could swing one leg over his and straddle him just as if he were her mount. His hands found her waist and settled there, anchoring her.

Vivi rose on her knees and stared down at him, the man she had adored as a girl and then loved as a woman. The man she had given herself to, the man she had married. In wonder, she touched him, cupping his face in both hands, feeling the new texture of his beard beneath her questing fingertips—springy yet sleek and soft. She found, too, the sharp line of his jaw. His eyes were on hers, holding her as tangibly as any tether. He was so handsome, so beloved. And she had missed him every moment he had been away.

But he was here now. He was firm and solid and muscled, his grasp on her waist tight, as if he feared she might pull away at any second and leave him. And then she said his name.

"Court."

She whispered it, half prayer, half sigh. For long before he had been the Duke of Bradford, that was how she had known him. It was what Percy had called him, how Vivi had always referred to him. His title felt wrong when they were together, as if he were a stranger.

He turned his head, kissed one palm, then the other. "Yes, sweetheart?"

"I missed you," she confessed. "I missed us."

"I missed you too." One of his hands left her waist to slide under her gown and undergarments, finding the stocking-covered skin of her bent knee. "I missed touching you. I missed your laughter, your smile. I missed looking at you and thinking how beautiful you are."

Her heart thudded painfully, hope burgeoning like a bud ready to unfurl into a blossom. "Why did you not come back sooner? Why wait so long if you missed me?"

The hand that had been traveling incrementally higher on her leg stilled. "I told myself that I owed him a year. A proper year of mourning."

Percy.

She had forever regretted the haste with which she and Court had wed— although marrying him was all she had ever wanted—and how close it had been to her brother's drowning. Gossip had swirled at the shocking haste; speculation over the reason had been rampant.

It occurred to her suddenly that Court had returned within days of the date he had left her one year before. So very close to the anniversary of their wedding. She had spent that particular day throwing herself into the planning for her house party and trying not to allow herself to think of him or long for him, to remember the day they'd wed, when she'd still been foolish enough to hope their marriage could be happy, despite the circumstances under which it had been made.

She traced Court's lips, her finger lingering on his philtrum. "We did everything wrong, didn't we?"

"Not everything, Vivi." His hand shifted, gliding higher, moving above her garters and setting her alight. "We married each other."

The sun was setting behind the castle walls, and they were comfortably enveloped in the cool shade of impending night. Birds chirped around them, and the scents of summer and Court were in the air. She wanted to bury her nose in his throat and inhale deeply, to lose herself in him.

But misgivings remained.

She searched his gaze, seeking answers and finding only more secrets and mysteries. For as many years as she had known Court, there remained so much she needed to learn.

"Was marrying each other the right thing to do?" she asked, rubbing her thumb slowly over his lower lip.

It was soft and full and so very warm.

He caught the pad of her thumb with his teeth, giving her a light nip. "It feels right, doesn't it?"

As he asked the question, he moved his hand the rest of the way up her thigh, the only barrier between them the fine linen of her drawers. Drawers that were damp from wanting him. If he touched her there, he would make that embarrassing discovery for himself.

"It feels right now," she admitted, "but it didn't feel right all the time you were away from me."

Time during which she had clung to those terrible words that had cut her like a knife.

A mistake.

"Nor for me," he murmured, his lips grazing her as he spoke. "Do you know how many nights I dreamed of having you this close?"

Likely as many as she had.

"Every. Damned. Night," he answered before she could utter a word.

"And yet, you continued on with your travels," she couldn't help but point out, for despite their proximity and the desire for him that made her so very vulnerable, the anguish of the last year remained, bitter and dark inside her heart.

Only time and Court proving himself to her would help her to heal.

"I had to distract myself." The hand on her waist gave a gentle, reassuring squeeze, while his other remained on her outer thigh, tempting and tormenting at once. "But I realized that what I was seeking was what I had left in England. You, Vivi. You're home to me. You're all I ever wanted. All I'll ever need."

She released her hold on his handsome face and locked her arms around his neck instead. And then she kissed him. Kissed him slowly, deeply. Kissed him as she had longed to do all the days they had been apart—and so many days before them, too. Thought fled. Emotions fell away. Need supplanted all else. And she took what she wanted.

Took his low groan of surrender, took his tongue into her mouth, the taste of him—sweet like wine and forbidden like sin—so delicious. A lusty sound escaped her, born of her frustration and desire. Their tongues tangled, and then his hand was twisted in the hair at her nape and hairpins were falling, and he moved his other hand yet again, finding the split in her drawers with expert ease and wicked intent.

The first brush of his fingers over her seam made Vivi's

hips buck and sent an electric current of pure, unadulterated pleasure straight through her. Oh dear God, she had forgotten how wonderful it felt to be touched there by someone other than herself. Tenderly, with painstaking care, he parted her folds, his fingers finding the sensitive knot within and swirling over it.

The breath rushed from her lungs. She kissed him harder, thrusting against his touch. Urging him wordlessly to give her more. As if sensing her need, he increased his speed, his touch flying over her with expert precision, playing her with the ease of a virtuoso. That splendid feeling was building inside her already, spurred on by the lonely nights she had spent without him and her body's undeniable reaction to him.

He was the first to break the kiss, relentlessly working her pearl, painting her with her own dew—so plentiful that her cheeks went hot with embarrassment. His lips were dark and glistening from her kisses, and his eyes had deepened to the mysterious shade of the ocean just after a storm.

"You're so wet for me," he murmured. "So hot and softer than silk. Just like I remembered."

He said it as if her eagerness was not a bad thing, and gratitude soared through her with the pleasure. His fingers worked her in tiny, mind-addling circles. She tried to respond, but she was already about to break, so instead, she laid her head on his shoulder and buried her face in his throat as she had been longing to do, inhaling deeply of his familiar scent.

"Come for me, Vivi," Court urged, his voice low and sinful and pure velvet. "Come on my fingers, sweetheart."

He was relentless. Knowing. When he increased the pressure and found a place that sent desire shooting up her spine, she lost control completely. On a gusty moan, she fell apart, grinding herself against his fingers as her orgasm shattered her.

As she pressed her face into the side of his neck and whispered his name in awe, that was when the first, fat droplets of rain spattered on her head.

And then, the deluge began.

CHAPTER 8

*B*y the time Court shouldered his way into the haven of her chamber, Vivi's teeth were chattering and the layers of her gown and undergarments were thoroughly sodden. She was dripping all over the Axminster, and she was sure she resembled nothing so much as a bedraggled cat who had fallen into a river.

"I am perfectly capable of walking," she protested for the fourth time since he had insisted upon carrying her from the stables, through the great hall, and up the grand staircase to her room.

He had ignored her every objection, storming through the manor house with her in his arms as if he were a knight of old.

"You're cold," he countered grimly, stalking to the fire that crackled in the grate.

Sherborne Manor was notorious for its chill, even in the height of summer. Thankfully, a servant had already seen the fire built for her comfort, for the rain had brought with it a decided burst of cold air. She and Court had frantically packed away the remnants of their picnic and sheltered in the ruins of the castle until the storm had passed. But the heaviness of the rain meant they had both been soaked before they had finally hidden away within the drafty castle's thick stone walls.

Her lady's maid came flying out of the small dressing area attached to Vivi's suite, her eyes going wide when she saw the spectacle they must have presented—long-lost husband and wife, both drenched.

"Your Graces!" Nelson exclaimed. "What has happened? Has Her Grace been injured?"

"I am fine," Vivi reassured the worried domestic. "We were merely caught in the rain, and the downpour was quite heavy."

"Please see that a hot bath is drawn for the duchess," Court told Nelson. "I'll help her with her garments."

The lady's maid dipped into a curtsy. "Of course, Your Grace."

She disappeared back into the dressing room, which possessed a door on the opposite end leading to the bathroom Vivi had recently seen renovated. Nelson had been with her for years, but it felt somehow odd to be in her bedchamber with Court this way in front of her lady's maid. Not wrong, for he was Vivi's husband. But slightly embarrassing. She shivered again, her teeth clacking together, as Court lowered her to the floor before the fire.

"Damn it, I have no wish for you to catch a lung infection," he muttered, his mouth still set in a firm, grim line.

"I have been caught in the rain before," she told him, though in truth, she was eager to be rid of her damp garments, which were sticking tenaciously to her skin. "I am certain all shall be well."

"Nonetheless, it is my fault we were stranded in the rain. If I had paid attention to the skies, I might have spared us the misery of all these blasted wet clothes." His hands settled on her waist in a proprietary fashion, and he spun her back toward the fire. "Warm yourself while I work on your dress."

"Nelson is accustomed to assisting me," she pointed out, disliking the notion of him helping her to disrobe.

For after those wild kisses in the castle bailey, and the way he had so easily and expertly brought her to release, she wasn't certain she trusted herself to maintain her restraint in his presence. He was hovering over her in proximity, and although he had held her in his arms and carried her here, there was something even more disturbingly intimate about standing face-to-face, knowing he intended to undress her.

"I'm certain she is," he said mildly, fingers at work on the fastenings of her gown.

He began at her throat, his knuckles grazing over the sensitive skin there, which was apparently as eager for his touch as the rest of her. She held her breath, hoping he wouldn't notice her reaction, and pinned her gaze to the buttons on his shirt above the vee of his tweed waistcoat. Her wet silk began to gape.

She could remain impervious, she told herself. What had happened earlier at the picnic had been an aberration, nothing more. All she had to do was send him away so that she could bathe in peace.

"You needn't help," she pointed out firmly, finding her voice. "You ought to go to your chamber and remove your own wet garments, lest you catch an ague yourself."

"Of course I need to help you." His baritone was a pleasant rumble that sent a new shiver over her that had nothing to do with her cold, wet gown and petticoats. "I've been remiss in my duties for far too long."

He had. She wouldn't argue on that score.

Her gown loosened further, her bodice opening to reveal her corset cover, which she had hand-embroidered herself with birds and roses, two of her favorites. He stilled, his gaze lifting from his task to meld with hers.

"Your work?" he asked, although she had no doubt he already knew the answer.

"Yes." Heat warmed her cheeks.

She felt unaccountably exposed to him, although he had done nothing more than unbutton her bodice three quarters of the way. But her corset cover was an undergarment, something only she and Nelson saw, and despite the fact that Court had seen all of her previously, the notion of him seeing her again was decidedly unsettling.

Because she wanted it more than she wanted anything else.

"It's beautiful." Lightly, he traced the pattern of birds and flowers directly over her madly thumping heart. "You were always skilled with a needle, and I know how much you adore roses and birds."

More facets he had noticed without her even being aware.

New warmth blossomed inside her. "Thank you."

She cursed herself for the sudden breathless quality of her voice as he reached the last button at her waist. With her bodice hanging limply in two wet halves, Court pulled her sleeves from her arms in smooth, efficient tugs. When it was completely removed, he draped it neatly over the back of a nearby chair before resuming his task.

He found the ties at her waist holding her skirts in place and undid them, sending the silk to the floor. "Corset cover next, I reckon."

Her fingers flew to the buttons. "I'll remove it myself."

But he gently knocked her hands to the side. "Let me tend you, Vivi."

She held herself stiffly as he resumed stripping her of her undergarments, all too aware of his nearness, his green-blue stare seemingly eating her up, and Nelson's presence in the distant bathing chamber. At any moment, she would return.

"I'm not accustomed to being attended by anyone other than Nelson," she murmured.

But her protest didn't give him pause.

He continued slipping buttons from their moorings. "As I said, I've been remiss in my duties."

Her corset cover was whisked away, placed atop her bodice. And then she stood before him in her red satin corset trimmed with black lace. She had ordered it because she had been feeling rebellious and daring, but it had been for her eyes alone. His gaze darkened, lingering on the way the undergarment's stiff boning lifted her breasts in a bold display.

"You look gorgeous in red," he said, his voice thick with suppressed desire as he ran his knuckles lightly over the curve of one breast, hidden from view by her thin chemise.

"The bath is ready, Your Grace," Nelson announced brightly as she reentered the room.

Vivi leapt away from Court guiltily, keeping her gaze averted to the fire. "Thank you, Nelson. His Grace was just leaving. Will you help me with the rest of my dress?"

"Actually," Court interceded smoothly, "I'll assist Her Grace with her garments and bath. You may go."

He was dismissing her lady's maid? For what purpose? She thought of the bath Nelson had prepared for her, and her alarm tripled. She couldn't allow Court to witness the humiliating fear that had been haunting her ever since Percy's death. What would he think? Nor did she trust herself to allow him to remove all her clothing.

"As you wish, Your Grace," Nelson said, the rustle of cloth indicating she was dipping into another curtsy. "Ring if you require anything else. I bid you good evening."

No, no, no.

Vivi couldn't be left alone with Court.

She spun about to stay Nelson, but the capable lady's maid was already disappearing from view on the other side of the door. It clicked softly closed at her back, leaving Vivi alone with her husband.

"Don't look so alarmed, sweetheart," Court said, taking her chin between his thumb and forefinger in a gentle hold and tilting her head so that she met his gaze. "Do you not trust yourself to be alone with me after what happened in the bailey?"

That was part of the problem, yes.

But there was also another, equally concerning hindrance.

"I trust myself well enough," she said crisply. "It is you whom I don't trust."

"I'll own that I haven't given you much reason to trust me yet. But I swear to you, Vivi, that I have no intention of hurting you or leaving you ever again."

His gaze was unwavering, burning into a part of her that was his alone.

"Very well," she relented. "You may help me to disrobe down to my chemise and drawers. But after that, I must insist you leave me to remove the rest and bathe myself."

He released his hold on her chin, his countenance turning contemplative. "I promise not to do anything you don't want."

It was what she wanted that Vivi feared. Because it was too much, too soon. And she longed for him more than she ever had.

But Court wasn't waiting for her response anyway. His agile fingers were already on the tapes of her petticoat, untying Nelson's knot.

"Forgive me for being wary of such a promise," she said wryly. "It sounds decidedly self-serving."

Not to mention, all too dangerous.

The knot loosened, and with a bit of help from Court, her ruffled petticoat fell to join her skirts, equally wet from the rain.

"You've caught me." He grinned at her, unfairly handsome, looking every bit the charming young man who had stolen her heart long ago. "That's because it *is* self-serving. I'll not lie, Vivi. I want to touch you. Everywhere and often. I want to explore every inch of you. To kiss you everywhere. To make you—"

"Hush," she interrupted, clapping her hand over his mouth to keep any further revelations from being made, for they were putting her determination in dreadful peril. "Not another wicked word out of you."

Because heaven help her if he said anything else. If he completed what he'd been about to say. She thought she knew.

To make you come.

Her sex throbbed at the thought of him visiting similar pleasure upon her again. Of how much she would like it. Of how desperate she would be for him to indeed touch and kiss her all over her weak and willing body.

He kissed her palm, making her tear her hand away, even as the action sent a jolt of longing straight to her core.

"I promise to behave myself," he said.

And Vivi didn't believe him. Not for one moment. Because Harcourt Sherborne, Ninth Duke of Bradford, had never behaved himself in any capacity, and she didn't expect him to begin now.

DOING his utmost to keep his raging desire for his wife under control, Court escorted Vivi to the bathroom adjoining her suite. Honoring her wishes, he had left her in her stockings, chemise, and drawers. Much of her mouthwatering skin had been bared to his hungry gaze, though still not enough. The state of his cock was a testament to how beautiful and tempting she was, given the hideously sodden fabric sticking to him everywhere. He was itching to tear it from his back and sink into the welcoming embrace of a hot bath himself.

The sight of her in that red satin corset with its black lace had made him instantly hard despite everything, and he'd been trying desperately to distract himself so that he could honor his word and play the gentleman. Helping her to take down her hair hadn't helped. He had always adored the long, wavy golden locks she kept restrained in neat buns and Grecian braids. It shone like pure gold in the sunlight, and it was even longer now than he remembered, trailing down her back to brush the top of her delectable derriere.

She stopped them at the threshold to the bathroom, her shoulders tense. "Thank you, Court. I'll see you tomorrow."

Disappointment curdled his gut. A part of him had hoped that their earlier interlude in the bailey had meant that she was softening toward him. That she might allow him back into her bed and, eventually, back into her heart. But it seemed that the ease that had fallen between them at the castle had been replaced by her iron-willed determination to keep him at bay.

He knew he owed her his patience and a thousand other favors. Still, now that he had returned and she was within reach, he wanted nothing more than to be the husband she deserved. In every sense.

"My steward wrote that you renovated the old bathing room here," he said, seeking to prolong his time in her presence. "Will you not allow me to see it?"

Her lips tightened, and he could tell she was about to argue.

"A quick peek inside, and then I'll leave you to your night," he cajoled.

She nodded, looking reluctant and wary.

God, he hated that, even if he knew the fault was purely his own.

"Very well," Vivi allowed. "One peek, nothing more."

He reached for the door, opening it to the warm steam and sweet scent rising from the prepared bathtub at the room's center. Court took in the tiled floor and walls, the intricately carved vanity and mirror, and couldn't deny that the transformation, like so many others she had created here at Sherborne Manor, was an excellent one.

"It's lovely, Vivi," he said, his gaze sliding over the tub again and finding a curious sight. "But where has all your bathwater gone? Perhaps the stopper became loose. I'll draw some more for you."

He moved toward the tub, intent on his cause.

"No," Vivi said, hastening after him and catching his sleeve, sounding frantic. "There's no need for you to do that."

Another two strides, and he was towering over the tub, and realization hit him, sudden and hard.

The water hadn't drained from the tub. There was just scarcely any water in it, the tub filled to a shallow depth of a few inches and no more. The stopper was firmly in place, and there were no sounds, nor any other signs suggesting water was actively slipping away.

"Why is it not filled?" he asked her quietly, sensing there was a reason by the way her countenance shifted, her already ivory skin growing even more pale.

Needing to know.

"Please go," she said quietly, distraught.

There was not a chance that he would leave her like this.

"Vivi, tell me," he urged.

"You promised."

But she looked so damned helpless, alone in her ivory chemise.

"I'll not go when you're in such a state," he told her. "Something is amiss, and I want to know what it is."

"It's the water," she blurted, her eyes gleaming in the gaslight.

And suddenly, instantly, he understood. Understood because he'd suffered the same crushing fears when he had traveled across the ocean after Percy's drowning.

"You're afraid of it," he guessed.

She bit her lip, looking conflicted, wrapping her arms around herself in a protective gesture. "Water makes me think of Percy. Of how he would have suffered. When the tub is too full, it haunts me. I feel as if I can't breathe, and my heart gallops. Nelson knows. She fills the tub with only as much water as I'll need for bathing."

Christ.

All this time he had been away, thinking himself the broken one, fearing he was all wrong for her, and he should have been here at her side, helping her to heal. Because he saw all too clearly now that Vivi was every bit as shattered inside as he was.

Without further thought, he stalked to the tub, turning the tap that called for hot water and letting it splash into the mostly empty basin. And then he turned back to her, plucking his own buttons from their moorings, shrugging his wet coat to the floor.

She watched him with wide eyes. "What are you doing, Court?"

He held her stare. "I'm getting into that tub with you, and I'm going to hold you in my arms and show you that you're safe with me. That I'll protect you always. That I—"

He had been about to say that he loved her, but he cut himself off, emotion churning inside him with a rawness that he didn't trust. This was only his second day home from abroad. There would be time aplenty for emotions, and he had promised himself that he would be patient with her.

"That you what?" she pressed, still lingering by the threshold, looking so bloody alone that he could scarcely bear to look at her.

"That I suffered from the same fear," he confessed instead. "I drank myself half to death when I crossed the ocean for the first time after Percy's drowning. But succumbing to our fears doesn't help us to overcome them. Facing them does."

Worry lined her face. "I don't know if I'm ready to face them."

He removed his waistcoat, toed off his boots, methodically stripping himself before her. "We'll do it together."

CHAPTER 9

*V*ivi stared at Court, drinking in the glory of his masculine frame as he stood next to the rapidly filling tub without a stitch to hide his body from her avid gaze. He had shed all his wet garments down to his smalls. She had thought for a moment that he might leave them on for modesty's sake. But then, his long fingers had been flying over the last of the buttons keeping him clothed, and he had dropped his damp smalls as well. He stood before her now, as perfectly chiseled as any antiquity.

But alive instead of fashioned from cold, lifeless marble. Oh, so very alive.

He was lean and strong, his chest broad, lightly dappled with dark hair that trailed down his flat stomach as if it were an arrow pointing directly to his cock. Good heavens, he was a beautiful man. Feeling wicked, she allowed her gaze to follow that arrow, finding him long and thick and stiff. She felt an answering ache between her legs, the lingering memory of how he had felt inside her.

And for a moment, she forgot her fear of the water. But then he turned off the tap and slung a long leg over the side of the basin and then the other. He was standing in the tub, waiting for her to join him.

Her mouth went dry.

Court extended his hand to her. "Come."

"I…" Her words trailed off, and she licked her lips, her errant gaze once more lingering on a certain portion of his anatomy that leapt to attention beneath her eager regard.

"You," he prompted gently.

What had she been saying? His nudity robbed her of the ability to speak. Her fear of water thieved her capacity to properly think. Altogether, she was lost.

"You're safe here with me," he said soothingly, his voice low and deep and poignantly familiar. "You can trust me, sweetheart. Take off the rest of your garments and place your hand in mine."

Could she trust him?

He had hurt her so badly.

And yet, now that he had returned, the same old Court she had always loved, it was growing more difficult by the moment to keep her protective walls from crumbling. He was an enemy marauder who had crossed her moat and crashed through her portcullis, and there was nothing to stop him now, save her surrender.

"I don't know if I can lower myself into water that's so deep," she admitted, eyeing the tub's glistening contents, swirling around his finely formed knees.

"You've never tried to do it with me before. I'll hold you, Vivi."

She shivered again, a chill passing over her now that she was away from the fire and still wearing her damp undergarments. Removing them would chase the chill. But where once she would have adored a deep, long soak in a tub, ever since Percy's death and the nightmares that had tormented her, her panic had rendered it impossible.

"Deep breaths," Court told her. "One step at a time. Take off your stockings and garters."

Her stockings were muddied and wet, and her feet were hopelessly cold. Bending, she obeyed, rolling down her garters and damp stockings under his watchful eye. When she finished and stood to find his heated gaze on her, some of the dread faded.

Deep breaths, she told herself, repeating Court's sage advice. *You can control this. You can overcome this.*

"You are strong, Vivi. So damned strong." His voice intruded on her wildly vacillating thoughts.

The fear receded slightly. She focused on Court's voice and realized she wanted to get into the tub. Wanted to fight her fear. To do so with him.

Before she lost her nerve, she caught her chemise in her hands and hauled it over her head, throwing the damp garment to the tiles at her feet. With scarcely any effort, she whisked her drawers away as well, and she was standing nude before her equally naked husband. It didn't feel wrong, nor did she feel any embarrassment. This was Court, the boy she had loved from afar for so long, turned into a man. And she was a woman. And perhaps, just perhaps, it was time to break free of the past.

"Come to me," he said.

One step. Then another. Closer, closer.

Her heart sped up, and her mouth was still dry and the fear threatened to intercede. But then she was there, within reach of his outstretched hand, and she placed hers in it. Their palms aligned. His eyes burned into hers.

He smiled, and it was the most tender smile she'd ever received from him. It was patient and gentle and partially hidden by his beard.

"I've got you, sweetheart," he promised.

And she believed him.

He helped her into the tub, the water hot at first, a shock to her cool skin.

She gasped, and he wrapped his arms around her, holding her to him. Although they were both naked and he was clearly not unaffected by her nudity, there was nothing sensual about his embrace. He was comforting her. Mooring her.

Vivi pressed her ear to his chest above his heart and inhaled slowly, trying to keep the encroaching alarm away. Listening instead to the steady, rhythmic thumps of Court's heart. Reminding herself that the water in which they stood wasn't the vast sea that had claimed her brother. Rather, it was nothing more than a vessel. One she had chosen herself even as she had known she was too fearful to use it properly.

But the fear was ebbing now.

Court moved his hands up and down her spine slowly as he kissed her crown. "There you are, my brave and beautiful wife. You've made it halfway."

His praise had her spine stiffening, for it was a reminder that he intended for them to become immersed in the bathwater together, something she hadn't done since Percy's drowning.

"I'm not sure I can make it the rest of the way," she admitted.

His hand continued its slow, comforting caress up and down her back.

"Do you remember when you climbed your first tree?" he asked, his voice rumbling beneath her ear.

She inhaled his scent, soap and Court, holding him tightly as she forced her mind back to that long-ago day. "I was afraid I would fall."

She had lingered at the base of the ancient oak for so long, staring up at the leafy boughs above and wishing herself amongst them. But she hadn't the strength to haul herself onto the lowest branch, weighed down by her heavy skirts.

"And who was there to tell you that you wouldn't?" Court asked.

"You."

Where Percy had laughed at her and gone off into a field with Alberta, Court had lingered. He'd knelt and offered her the use of his thigh as a stool.

"I'm still here, Vivi," he said.

She swallowed hard, thinking about her brother and the unfairness of his life cut so swiftly and brutally short. Court was here. Percy was not. And she forced herself to think of the rest of what had happened, then. How Court had grasped her waist when she'd placed her boot on his manly thigh, half perishing with embarrassment and unrequited love for him, and he'd caught her waist in an easy grasp, helping her to reach the lowest branch.

"You helped me," she said softly, her fingers moving over the taut, bare skin of his lower back, relishing the feel of him.

"Let me help you again. We'll sit together on the count of three." He pressed another kiss to her head, almost reverently. "Ready, sweetheart?"

"No," she said, clutching him tightly, panic pushing the pleasant memory aside and making her chest go tight.

"Deep breaths," he reminded gently. "You can do it. One." He kissed her again, nothing more than the comforting brush of his lips over her part, and yet it meant so much, the gesture so painfully tender and caring that she might have wept were her demons not so intent on chasing her. "Two."

"Court," she protested, sinking her fingernails into his back. "Not yet."

She was thinking about Percy. About the yacht sinking in that terrible storm, how terrified he must have been. Thinking about his final moments. Had he gone down with the ship, or had he struggled to swim to shore, only to sink below the waves and disappear forever? And what had that felt like, losing his ability to breathe…

"Come back to me, Vivi." Court's stern, beloved voice tore her from her agonizing thoughts as he continued to caress up and down her spine. "Stay with me. Right here, in this moment. Can you do that for me?"

She wanted to.

A shudder went through her, and she was cold. So cold. She shivered, trembled, longed to surround herself in the welcoming heat of the bathwater.

Not the ocean, she reminded herself, closing her eyes tightly. *I'm with Court. I'm safe.*

"Yes," she gasped out. "I can do it."

"Good," he crooned, stroking her hair now. "Three."

And then, he was guiding them both down, into the bath. Everything became a blur of light and sound and fear, and she scrambled to fight him, but he was stronger and he overcame her with ease. They sank together, Court resting on the bottom of the tub with Vivi atop him, much as it had been earlier during their bailey picnic.

She was gasping for breath, and yet she had done it. She was here. Submerged to her chin and wrapped in Court's strong arms, her face tucked into his throat.

"You did it, sweetheart." He kissed her forehead. "You're in the bath with me."

Relief washed over her, joining the warmth, and miraculously, the fear began to recede. She trembled against him, overwhelmed by the virulence of her reaction.

She tipped her head back, meeting his gaze, love for him and joy colliding with the lingering old panic he had helped her to overcome. He cupped her cheek reverently, simply staring down at her as the bath warmed them both. She was thankful she had selected such a large tub, though certainly she had not done so with this in mind. And yet, how much better it was to share her bath with Court than to sit in her three inches of water alone.

"Just like the tree," she murmured, overwhelmed by the day, by Court's return, by her feelings for him.

"Just like the tree," he agreed, and then he lowered his lips to hers and kissed her with slow, thorough sweetness until she was whimpering into his mouth and one of her hands had strayed to his nape, curling into the too-long strands there.

This kiss was different from the voracious meeting of mouths they had shared earlier. It was softer, more tender. It was deliberate and careful, and yet it was a seduction so thorough that she never wanted her mouth to leave his. She wanted to wrap herself around him, to hold him close, to never let him go.

Beneath her bottom, the undeniable thick prod of his cock coming back to life sent a pulse of need to her sex. He deepened the kiss, the pressure of his mouth growing more insistent, his tongue at last teasing the seam of her lips. And she opened for him with a helpless sound, wanting to forget everything but him. The past, the present, the future.

She didn't want to think about the pain he'd caused her, about the reasons they'd spent the last year apart. Didn't want to think about the looming house party, or the dozens of guests she was about to receive. All she wanted to concentrate on was Court.

Her husband, her friend, the man she had never stopped loving.

Her body moved with a purpose all its own, and she was gliding in the water, settling so that she was astride him, with his cock nestling against her aching folds. Shamelessly, she kissed him as she rocked her hips, craving the most intimate joining of all.

He was first to break the connection, his lips leaving hers to travel along her jaw, down her throat.

"Vivi," he murmured her name against her skin as if it were a prayer. "My sweet, gorgeous, bold Vivi. I've been lost without you."

What could she say to that? For her, it had been the same. She had buried herself in tasks as a means of distraction. She had thrown herself into restoring the gardens at Sherborne Manor and renovating the bathrooms. She had immersed herself in the Lady's Suffrage Society and in her growing group of friends. But one thing had been missing from her life, and it was Court.

His mouth traveled along her throat, and he pressed a kiss to the hollow at the base, then trailed more across her collarbone, following it to the curve of her bare shoulder. One of his hands cupped her breast, his thumb stroking over her hard nipple, sending sensation shooting through her.

She clutched at his muscled upper arm for purchase in the slippery tub, deciding he should not be the only one exploring. Her other hand trailed down his chest, then lower, dipping under the water. She waited for the fear to intrude, for the panic to assail her, and yet this time, it did not. Because she was not alone and her body was humming with reawakened need. Her fingers trailed down his abdomen until she found what she was looking for, and they curled around his thick, heavy length.

"Fuck, Vivi," he muttered as she stroked him with a tight grasp he'd shown her before. "You'll unman me."

His words, coupled with his soft groan and the way he hardened beneath her touch, spurred her on. She sought his mouth, kissing him again, their tongues writhing against each other, the meeting of lips turning wet and carnal as her hand moved on his lengthening shaft below the water. He plucked at her nipple, rolling it between his thumb and forefinger, before giving it a soft pinch that sent exquisite pleasure unfurling through her. The persistent ache between her thighs intensified as he fed her voracious kisses and plundered her mouth.

They parted for air, their breathing ragged, and he caught her wrist in a gentle grip, disengaging his cock from her grasp. "No more, or I'll not last. This isn't what I intended when I invited you into the bath."

"I suppose we should bathe before the water grows too cold," she agreed, although she wanted nothing more than to continue touching him, kissing him.

"We should." He kissed her again, swift and hard, as if he couldn't resist.

They made short work of washing each other using the soap and shampoo Nelson had left for her, before rinsing and rising from the bath to soft towels. They dried themselves, and then Court took her hand, wordlessly guiding her from the bathroom, through her dressing room, to the bedchamber.

"Sit, and I'll brush your hair," he said, gesturing toward the chair positioned before her mirror, where Nelson had also laid out her hairbrush.

With the towel wrapped around her, their shared bath leaving her warm and relaxed, she did as he requested, staring at her reflection, Court hovering over her, a solid presence at her back. His towel hung low on his hips, and she couldn't help but admire his broad, bare shoulders and his muscled chest. He took up the brush and slowly ran its bristles through her wet hair. The steady, rhythmic strokes calmed her.

"That feels lovely," she admitted, trying not to sigh in contentment.

"I've always loved your hair," he said, taking her by surprise.

"You have?"

He'd certainly never told her as much.

"Mmm," he murmured, working the brush through her wet tangles. "It's like sunshine on a flawless summer day, golden and bright."

Was he trying to woo her? Because if so, it was working. Her anger and bitterness were steadily being burned to ash by the flames of desire. *Mere days*, she reminded herself. *He has only been home for days after a year's absence.*

"I always wished I had dark hair like Clementine," she said, trying to keep her mind occupied so that her body's restless yearning might be quelled.

"Lady Clementine has dark hair? I couldn't see it under that monstrosity of a hat."

"She does, and it's beautiful." Vivi couldn't seem to look away from the mirror, from the sight of Court standing handsome and strong behind her, gently guiding the brush through her hair. "Mine is pale and boring."

"I can assure you that nothing about you is boring," Court said, his gaze lifting to meet hers in the mirror. "And you are perfect exactly as you are."

"Far from perfect," she denied, but his praise sent warmth cascading through her just the same.

"I'll not hear otherwise." He swept her hair to one side, leaving her throat exposed.

Holding her stare, he pressed a kiss to the place where her neck and shoulder met.

Her determination melted.

"Court." His name left her, and she wasn't sure whether it was in protest or plea.

"Do you want me to stay, Vivi?" He kissed her throat, the sight mesmerizing. "Or do you want me to go?"

How could she want him to go when his mouth was on

her skin? It was unfair, the effect he had on her. The way he made her feel.

"Stay," she said.

⁓

A SURGE of desire so overwhelming that it almost knocked him on his arse hit Court at that one word. *Stay.* He closed his eyes and remained as he was, face buried in Vivi's neck, the flutter of her pulse beating fast beneath his lips. He'd been too afraid to hope that she would want him. Christ knew he wanted nothing but her. Had longed for her every day he'd been gone from her side.

"Thank God." Throat thick with pent-up desire, he straightened to his full height and replaced the brush on the polished mahogany.

She rose from her chair and turned to face him, her beauty robbing him of breath. It wasn't just that Vivi was lovely, although it was undeniable that she was. Rather, it was the fact that his self-imposed isolation was finally at an end and that somehow, miraculously, she was allowing him back into her life. Willingly, and not out of a sense of obligation or duty.

He understood that her acquiescence didn't mean that everything between them would return to the way it had been before, but this was a step in the right direction, and one he was damned thankful for. They could find their way together. Being her husband, being with her, freed of the mantle of guilt he'd been wearing for so long, was new to him as well.

Court laced his fingers through hers and led her to the bed. When they reached it, he turned her to face him. "You're certain, Vivi?"

She gave him a nod. "Yes."

His cock, still half hard from her hand on him in the bath, rose thick and heavy. He swallowed, unwinding the towel from around her as if he unwrapped a present, for that was what she was to him. A gift he didn't deserve, but one that was his alone. His to savor, to protect, to love. The old guilt threatened to rise, but he tamped it viciously down.

His period of mourning his best friend was done, and he had to believe that Percy would understand had he still been here. Court couldn't deny his heart any longer. He'd been in love with Vivi for years, and for years, he had kept his distance, but the time for that was done.

Her towel fell from his limp fingers as he gave himself a moment to drink in the sight of her, flushed from the heat of their bath, her wet hair glistening in the lamplight. Her breasts were full and high, her curves made for his hands. He had never seen a more inviting sight.

She gave him a small smile, surprising him by hooking her fingers in his towel and tugging. "My turn to look my fill."

He allowed her to do as she wished, the towel dropping to the Axminster and joining hers. The trail of her hands over his shoulders and chest, the wonderment in her gaze, had his prick pulsing, and he was already leaking. Court caught her fingers before they could venture any farther.

"On the bed, sweetheart," he said. "I want to make love to you properly."

Vivi didn't protest. She lay down on the bed, holding his stare as she held her arms out to him. With a growl of pure, animalistic need, he joined her, guiding her legs apart so that he could settle himself between them. He was instantly distracted by her pink, glistening cunny. In the frantic moments of the boathouse, he'd been too moved by emotion and blinding need to take note of much more than her scent and how good it had felt to be deep inside her, claiming the woman who had always been his. He intended to take his time now, to savor, to make this night even more memorable than their first.

With a hand that trembled with suppressed emotion and desire, he caressed her inner thigh, lightly at first, just above her knee. Then higher, to where her beckoning heat called him. And though he had pleasured her earlier on the picnic blanket at Lynwood Castle, touching her now was every bit as heady. She was wet and sleek and hot, the scent of her, soap and musky woman, rising to tease his senses. He slicked her dew over her pearl, playing with the swollen bud until she made a low sound in her throat, hips pumping against him.

And suddenly, he couldn't wait. He replaced his fingers with his lips, kissing her, then lightly flicking his tongue over her as she moaned and writhed under him. The taste of her was on his tongue—sweet and musky as her scent—and fucking hell, he couldn't get enough. He sucked and licked, devouring her, lost in her as he leveraged himself on a forearm and grasped her hip.

Above him, his name emerged from her as a strangled cry.

"Court." She made a sharp inhalation of breath as his fingers returned to her, finding her entrance and slipping inside. "Oh yes. Please."

She was drenched, the tight walls of her cunny clinging to his finger as he pleasured her with his tongue. He sank inside to the hilt, enjoying the sensation of her wrapped around the lone digit, her inner muscles clamping down hard. Being inside her again was going to be so damned good. He could scarcely wait.

But he wanted her to come first. Wanted her helpless with desire, writhing and ready and even wetter than she already was. Teasing her with the very tip of his tongue as he sank a second finger deep inside her, Court looked up. She was glorious, pupils dilated, cheeks pink, full, kiss-stung lips parted, her hair a golden tangle around her on the pillow.

He left her clitoris for only a moment to murmur, "Watch me make you come."

And then he was a man intent again, kissing and licking and sucking, fucking her with his fingers. Rubbing his beard against her folds and inner thighs until she was squirming and gasping. Curling his fingers inside her and giving her bud a little nip.

"Oh dear heavens, I'm going to... It's too much," she said, gasping when he probed deeper, faster, sucking hard as he did so. "Court..."

Her words trailed away. He was intent on wringing an orgasm from her. He applied himself with renewed vigor, his rhythm finding the time of her dancing hips, his tongue and lips working over her until even he was thrusting his hips, grinding his aching cock into the mattress in an effort to stay his impending orgasm.

Her body bowed from the bed, and she clamped down on him as her release tore through her. He lingered as long as he dared, lapping at her with languid licks, loving the taste of her on his tongue, the way she thrust herself against his face like an offering, his fingers gliding in and out of her, wetness trailing down his wrist.

Until he couldn't wait another moment and withdrew, aligning his body with hers. His cock was slick from his seed, but he rubbed it through her folds in quick strokes that had them both moaning at the sheer pleasure of the sensation. When they had made love in the boathouse, she'd been a virgin. He had caused her some pain, he knew, and he'd be damned if he hurt her a second time. He wanted her prepared, ready. Grasping himself, he ground his cock head against her clitoris, torturing them both some more as he sucked one of her dusky-pink nipples into his mouth.

She opened her legs wider in wordless invitation. One he accepted, guiding himself to her cunny. She felt so good, beckoning him with her heat and her wetness. Like home. Like his. Like everything he'd ever wanted and hadn't dared to claim.

He thrust forward, her nipple popping from his mouth as he let out a groan of pure, unadulterated pleasure. Her body clamped down on him, threatening to force him out. So he thrust again, deeper, not stopping until he was seated to the hilt. He was inside her, surrounded by her, and the need to come was already roaring through him like a wildfire.

"Oh," she breathed.

"Ah God, Vivi." He stayed as he was for a moment, struggling to regain control, kissing the curve of her breast. "You feel so good."

Better than good. What a stupid, insufficient bloody word to describe the euphoria soaring through his veins. Nothing had ever felt better, nor more right. He was exactly where he belonged.

"You feel wonderful," she murmured, clinging to him as if she feared he would go if she released her hold on him.

Not a fucking chance.

He found a rhythm that began as tender before he swiftly lost control and became relentless. They met each other thrust for thrust, faster and faster, both of them moving together as if they had been made for lovemaking. She was making soft, needy sounds of surrender that were driving him to the brink, her hands on him everywhere. He kissed her hard, feeding her the taste of herself on his tongue. His fingers slipped between them, to where their bodies joined, and he rubbed her pearl until she stiffened and cried out, her orgasm thundering through her. She tightened on his cock, and he plunged faster, fucking her up the mattress in his frenzy, until he couldn't avoid his release for another second. He sank his cock deep one last time, and pleasure rolled up his spine as he came, filling her with his seed just as he had spent the last year dreaming of.

Only this time, it was real, and as he collapsed to the bed at Vivi's side, he threw an arm around her waist, pulling her close to him. Burying his face in the damp cloud of her golden hair, he fell into the soundest sleep he'd had in just as long.

CHAPTER 10

"*I* do believe I've never seen you looking so content," Clementine told Vivi as they strolled along the gravel pathway in the gardens, late-afternoon sunlight streaming around them.

"I'm sure I don't look like anything but a woman about to be inundated with houseguests," she demurred.

Content.

Was that the word for what she was feeling inside, the warm glow that suffused her whenever Court was near or merely in her thoughts?

Part of her hated to think it was, because contentedness terrified Vivi where he was concerned. The past fortnight had been a blur of preparations for the house party and getting reacquainted with her husband.

In every sense.

Most particularly, the sense involving a bed. And sometimes, a door. And other times, a chaise longue. Once, on a blanket spread out in the abandoned castle bailey where they'd had their picnic. But enough of that. Vivi's cheeks were growing hot beneath her friend's knowing scrutiny.

"And now, you're blushing," Clementine added, grinning.

She was, and she hated it.

"I'm not," she lied archly. "You are simply hoping to have another matchmaking victory, my dear."

"Can I be the matchmaker when the two of you are already married, however?" her friend asked with feigned innocence.

Vivi knew quite well that Clementine had been throwing Court and Vivi together at every opportunity. A group walk to the river when she pleaded a headache at the last moment, leaving Court and Vivi to go alone. An offer to aid with the final details of lawn chess, only to be conspicuously absent, Court there in her place. Taking dinners in her room. Disappearing from the breakfast table. Clementine had any number of matchmaking tricks at her disposal, and she had no qualms about employing them all.

Vivi didn't entirely mind. Being alone with Court was no hardship, even if every moment that passed in his presence left her falling even more deeply in love with him. In some ways, it was as if no time had passed at all and they had simply taken up where they had left off in the boathouse. And yet, in other ways, it was as if they were discovering each other anew. It was terrifying and exhilarating, all at once. Rather like climbing a tree—triumph from the boughs even as she feared a fatal slip would send her crashing down.

"If not matchmaking, what would you call your invitation to examine the constellations in the night sky and subsequent failure to appear, leaving Court and me alone to view the stars?" Vivi asked her friend pointedly.

"I would call it falling asleep before I was able to meet you both." Clementine defended herself airily. "Preparing for a country house party is terribly tiring."

"Ha," Vivi scoffed, not believing her friend's denial for a

moment. "You forget how well I know you. You're never abed before half past one in the morning."

"The Venus fountain is looking decidedly lovely," Clementine said, neatly changing the subject as they rounded a bend and the repaired fountain came into view, water gurgling cheerfully from the lion heads and cherubs decorating its base.

Originally commissioned in the late seventeenth century, the fountain had been in a terrible state of disrepair, with pipes broken in the ground that had required replacing. A statue of Venus emerging from her bath, a towel draped before her, towered from above. It was, undeniably, magnificent. Shipley had painstakingly organized the repairs and had resodded the lawn around the sunken fountain, leaving the observer none the wiser that it had once sat mildewed and empty and sad.

"Yes, it is," Vivi agreed, proud of the fountain's new life but still not willing to be derailed, "and you are also abysmal at attempting to redirect the conversation."

"I was hardly redirecting," Clementine said with a sniff. "I was merely observing and admiring. Just as you do with your husband."

Her cheeks went hotter still, and she couldn't deny her friend's observation, for it was true. If Court was in a room, her eyes inevitably landed on him. The more time she spent with him, the more he charmed her, the more he touched and kissed and made love to her, the less she could resist him. But then, she had always worn her heart on her sleeve where Court was concerned. Time had carried on, but her feelings for him had never altered.

"Do take care, or I'll set Lady Featherstone upon you when she arrives," Vivi cautioned lightly.

There was no sting in her voice, nor did she have any intention of following through on her threat. She wouldn't set the marchioness on her greatest enemy, let alone her dearest friend.

Clementine held a hand over her heart in dramatic fashion. "Perish the thought. I can still scarcely believe you invited the wretched woman."

"She isn't always wretched," Vivi said, grinning. "When she is sleeping, for instance, the marchioness is perfectly pleasant."

Clementine chortled. "And even in her slumber, she is likely haranguing some poor, unsuspecting person. I would wager she dreams of issuing setdowns."

Vivi couldn't contain her own chuckle at the notion of the dowager reprimanding imaginary debutantes in her sleep. "And no doubt frightening kittens and puppies as well."

They stopped before the fountain, Venus high on her pedestal above.

"Good heavens, are those little men...urinating?" Clementine asked, sounding horrified at the prospect, but also amused.

The fountain's designer had indeed cleverly equipped the four Cupids ringing the lower tier of the fountain with miniature members from which a spout of water poured endlessly forth.

"They are." Vivi chuckled again, relieved for the distraction of their earlier conversation. "Quite clever, is it not?"

Clementine was frowning at the nearest Cupid's stream. "Please tell me not all gentlemen are so poorly equipped."

Vivi nearly choked. "Clementine!"

"What?" Her friend sent her an unrepentant look. "You can hardly fault a lady for being curious, can you? I was merely taking note that the fellow's manhood seemed dreadfully small in proportion to the rest of his anatomy."

She groaned. "Promise me that you won't say anything so untoward within hearing range of Lady Featherstone. Lady

Edith will never be permitted to join the Lady's Suffrage Society."

"I promise not to talk about Cupid's tiny manhood in front of the dragon marchioness," Clementine said with mock severity.

Vivi sighed. "Somehow, that scarcely sounds reassuring."

Clementine sent her a bright smile. "Never fear, Vivi. I'll not ruin your house party or our chances of persuading Lady Edith to join our cause. Now, you must tell me about everything that has happened between you and Bradford. I've been hoping you would volunteer the information, but my curiosity cannot bear waiting another second longer."

Vivi didn't even know where to begin. The past fortnight had been a dream. And yet, she found herself perpetually waiting for something to change, for her happiness to be wrestled away from her. For Court to leave again.

She looked away from Clementine's probing blue stare, glancing pensively up at Venus. "Everything has happened, it seems."

Everything except for a declaration of love.

Vivi couldn't tamp down her disappointment at the reminder.

"The reason for your estrangement," Clementine began delicately. "I assume it has been resolved?"

She sighed, turning back to her friend. "Not entirely. Apparently, my brother demanded a promise from him to keep his distance from me, which he did. But after Percy died, we were both overwrought. He broke his promise, of course, and although it necessitated our marriage, his guilt was eating him alive."

Clementine gave her arm a gentle, comforting squeeze. "Oh, Vivi. I am so very sorry. I know how much you loved your brother. And he and Bradford were like brothers as well. How terrible it must have been for Bradford to be torn between two people he so dearly loved."

Her friend's words sent a surge of yearning through Vivi that she couldn't contain. "He loved Percy dearly, of course. As for me…"

"As for you?" Clementine prompted, her brow rising.

"Well." She paused, sighing again before summoning a smile. "I think that Bradford cares for me very much. But I doubt that he loves me. He's certainly never said so."

"He loves you," Clementine said firmly. "He may not have confessed it to you yet, but trust my matchmaker's instincts. A man does not look at a woman the way the duke looks at you without being hopelessly, helplessly in love. It certainly explains how conflicted he was. Imagine losing your best friend and then feeling powerless to tell the woman you love how you feel because of a promise you made him."

"He vowed to keep his promise for a full year of mourning," Vivi agreed. "His sense of honor wouldn't allow for anything less. But that doesn't mean he's in love with me. It has always been my fondest wish that one day he would be. Over time, however, I've had to accept that he may never return my tender feelings. Such is the way of life."

"Have you told him how you feel?" Clementine asked shrewdly. "You love him, do you not?"

She did. She had always loved Court, and nothing and no one—not time, not a year of heartache, not a promise to her brother—could change that. She was inextricably bound to him.

"He is the only man I have ever wanted," she admitted quietly. "Being his wife was the future I hoped for. But then when we married as we did, out of necessity to avoid scandal, and he left me, everything was ruined. All my hopes were dashed to bits. And my heart…"

"You're afraid to trust in him again, aren't you?" her friend asked sagely.

She nodded. "I'm afraid he'll break my heart a second time, and that it will be incapable of healing. The power he has over me terrifies me, Clementine."

"I understand." Clementine took Vivi's hands in hers. "In your shoes, I would also be wary. But he has come back to you, and he seems to be a man on a mission. And that mission is winning your heart."

Court, in love with her?

Vivi was too afraid to hope it was true, for it was all she had ever wanted.

She shook her head. "I just keep thinking of ways this all might have gone differently. If only I hadn't planned a house party. If only he had told me his reason for leaving before he left. And if only he had told me he would return."

"We can't live our lives by 'if onlys,' dear heart," Clementine said sensibly. "We must live them by certainties, with hope for the future."

"Why must you be so wise?" she asked, a note of teasing creeping into her voice.

Once more, she was heartily glad for her friend's presence here, for her listening ear, her sound advice.

Clementine winked. "All the best matchmakers are wise beyond their years."

Vivi bustled toward Court in the great hall, smelling of lush flowers and summer sunshine. She was so gorgeous, so beloved, so *his*, that an ache formed in his throat as he drank in the sight of her.

"I've been looking for you," she told him, a welcoming

smile on her lips that a mere fortnight ago he wouldn't have believed would ever be directed at him.

He wasn't sure that he deserved it.

They had come a long way in the last two weeks. But Court didn't fool himself. The wounds of the past year had not, by any means, been entirely healed, and he had yet to tell her the full truth of his guilt at Percy's drowning. But they had settled into an easiness with each other that had been absent since that night at the boathouse, and he was damned thankful for it.

"You've been looking for me, have you?" He stopped before her, tempted to kiss her pretty pink lips despite the likelihood of an audience.

Servants were everywhere, making final preparations for the arrival of the guests.

He narrowly resisted.

"Yes." Her blue gaze dipped to his mouth as if she were having similar thoughts. "I was wondering if the repairs on the west wing roof have been completed."

"They have," he confirmed. "The green chamber will be suitable for Lady Featherstone's impending occupation on the morrow."

Vivi's smile deepened. "Thank heavens. I was beginning to fear we would have to place her somewhere else, and that could have been disastrous."

"I'm pleased to be the savior of the house party," he said teasingly.

In truth, he wished there were no house party looming over them. After a year of self-imposed exile, he selfishly wanted his wife to himself. He wouldn't deny it. The very notion that he was about to have his ancestral home filled with guests for the next two weeks made his necktie feel like a hangman's noose. But Vivi had planned the affair, and he owed her far more than the indulgence of a fortnight's worth of merriments.

Vivi's countenance turned serious, her gaze burning into his. "I'm glad you are here, Court."

Simple words, but the meaning behind them was far more complex.

"I'm glad I am here as well," he managed past the emotion threatening to choke him.

How had he been able to survive a year without her? He never wanted to be away from her side again. But if they were to truly make amends and move beyond the pain of the past year, he needed to be completely honest with her.

He offered her his arm. "Walk with me?"

Her hand settled familiarly in the crook of his elbow. "Dare I ask where we are going?"

"To my bedroom," he answered quietly, keeping his voice from carrying to the busy domestics darting about the great hall.

Her fingers tightened on his sleeve, and she cast him a sidelong glance. "In the midst of the afternoon?"

The sinner in him wondered if she would object to such an assignation. But his intent was not, in this instance, carnal in nature.

"There is something there that I want to give you," he explained, thinking of the singing bird box that had finally arrived that morning from London.

He had sent the collections he had gathered in his travels separately, not realizing that they would be so delayed in their arrival. Thankfully, nothing had been damaged, and all the pieces had arrived in excellent condition.

"How mysterious," she said, matching his strides as they reached the staircase, beginning their ascent.

"By necessity," he quipped. "If I tell you what it is, the surprise will be spoiled."

"I am more curious than ever."

"You've always been curious, Vivi."

A strange sensation filled his chest as they went up the stairs together, and Court had to blink at the surprising sting of tears threatening to fall. Tears of gratitude that he was here at last, with the woman he loved at his side. That she had lowered her guard enough to allow him back into her life, into her bed, and, God willing one day, back into the most important place of all: her heart.

"I suppose I have," she allowed grudgingly. "Particularly where you are concerned, it would seem."

She said the last reluctantly, as if the admission cost her greatly. But Court was pleased by the revelation.

"Is that why you were always spying on Percy and me when we were trying to swim?" he teased, just to watch her cheeks turn pink.

She didn't disappoint him; Vivi averted her gaze, a becoming flush stealing over her creamy skin as they reached the top of the stairs.

They had known each other for so long. Vivi had been a spirited girl of fourteen when they had met, a hoyden who was never far from her brother's side. When Court had entered their lives, Vivi and Percy had welcomed him in a way his own family never had. His father had been icy and aloof, uninterested in his son aside from the annual interviews the duke conducted between affairs with opera singers and actresses. Mother had been scarcely better, seemingly suffering his presence as a duty. With Percy and Vivi, Court had laughed, adventured, and grown into a man.

Then had come the day that Vivi had matured into a beautiful young woman, and everything had changed. He'd been a careless rakehell in his day, but from the moment he had seen Vivi across the ballroom after her debut, no other woman had ever compared. He understood now that no woman ever could. She was his, and he was hers.

He could only hope like hell that she might one day return that love, or that, at the very least, he hadn't ruined their future by allowing himself to be weighed down by the past, his sense of honor, and a promise that he never bloody well should have made to Percy in the first place. Friend or not, he ought to have told Percy to go to the devil when he'd demanded the promise from him to stay away from Vivi.

Court couldn't change the past. But he could forge a future with Vivi—the future they both deserved.

"You are quite wretched to remind me of that," she said tartly, recovering her self-possession with remarkable speed as they passed through the picture gallery on their way to his chamber.

"I do believe we caught you on no fewer than five occasions," he couldn't resist adding. "At the time, I thought you were merely nettled that we didn't invite you to swim with us. Now, I wonder if there was perhaps another reason."

Vivi's spying had begun a few years into his friendship with Percy and subsequent visits to their country house. He reckoned she would have been about seventeen at the time.

"Hush," she said, looking about for servants, the tips of her ears even pink now. "Someone will hear you, and my dignity shall never recover."

Court chuckled as they reached his chamber, grateful for the momentary lightness between them, which would necessarily be banished as soon as he said what he had to say. His gut clenched at the thought. He had to hope there would be forgiveness for him in her heart.

That she wouldn't entirely hate him.

He opened the door, gesturing for her to precede him. She swept over the threshold and into the room that didn't feel like his and perhaps never would. Unlike many of the areas in Sherborne Manor, this chamber had gone untouched by Vivi. He hadn't yet thought to ask her why, but the question rose now, with the two of them alone in the afternoon light sifting through the windows.

"You didn't alter this chamber," he observed, studying her expressive face.

"No," she agreed quietly. Sadly. "I didn't."

"The reason?" he dared to ask.

"It was my fondest hope that you would return one day and make it your own," she said, looking pensive. "And now, here you are."

"Here I am," he repeated, wishing the barriers between them didn't feel so insurmountable. When they made love, time, past pain and heartache, guilt and grief were suspended. But their days were a waterfall of memories. And there remained the soul-deep guilt eating at him still. "I hope you don't regret it."

"I could never regret you being here with me," she said. "It is all I have wanted this last year, the chance to be your wife."

Her words stunned him. For a heartbeat, Court could do nothing other than stare at her, this gorgeous woman he had once promised his best friend he would never touch. This woman who was now his wife.

And then he was moving, retrieving the small box from atop his dresser where he had left his gift, turning back to her. "This is for you."

He offered it to her, feeling slightly foolish now, hoping she would recall the significance. It had been some ten years since she had lost the box in the library fire at Edmonds House.

Vivi accepted the parcel, unwrapping it slowly. When she extracted the tortoiseshell box, she gasped.

"Court. Surely it is not…" Her eyes flew to his, glistening with unshed tears.

He swallowed hard against a rising lump of emotion and gave a jerky nod. "It is. You had wondered at my interactions with the Marchioness of Hazlehurst in Paris. She is well-known for her collection of *objets d'art*. I had heard she was in possession of a singing bird box just like the one Percy gifted you years ago."

"You remembered," she said, a tear rolling down her cheek now.

"I know that you treasured it because Percy gave it to you, and this can never replace the box you lost," he began, moved by her reaction more than he was prepared to admit, "but I hope that you look upon it and that it brings you happy memories."

"Oh, Court." More tears were falling, and she made no move to stay them.

"Open it," he suggested, terrified he would unman himself by beginning to weep as well.

She sniffed, dashing at her cheeks with the back of her hand before pressing the lever on the front of the box. The lid popped open, the bird emerging with its little song, beak, wings, and tail all moving in delighted unison. When the song was done, the lid snapped closed.

"Thank you," she said with great feeling. "This is like receiving it from Percy, in a way, anew. I will treasure it always."

He sniffed, his eyes burning, vision blurring. Damn it, he hadn't wept in months. Drowning his misery in bottles of wine had seemed so much less painful.

"You needn't thank me," he forced himself to say, "particularly after you hear what I have to tell you."

She blinked, her head cocking in the fashion of an inquisitive bird as she held the box before her like a shield. "What is it that you have to tell me?"

He took a deep breath, summoning the courage to say the

words that he'd yet to acknowledge to anyone else. To reveal the true depths of the guilt that had been festering in his soul for the last year.

"I should have been with him when he set out from Ilfracombe on the *Marguerite*," he forced out, the admission painful, like a cracked and bruised rib. "The day he died."

Her brow furrowed. "What do you mean?"

God, he hated this. Hated saying the words, hated knowing that he could have been there for his friend. That he could have done something to help Percy when the yacht had begun to sink. But he had to tell Vivi. For himself, for her, for the brother and friend they had both so loved. The full truth was necessary.

"Percy was keen to test the yacht for the Cowes Regatta," he continued. "As you know, I was with him on that trip down to Devon."

She nodded. "We were grateful you were there to search for him after the *Marguerite* capsized."

Court had searched the unforgiving waters of the Bristol Channel for any sign of his best friend. But hours had passed, and while the bodies of the other men aboard had gradually been found, Percy's had never surfaced.

"What you don't know, and what I never told you, is that Percy had invited me to go with him on the yacht that morning. I had every intention to do so, but the night before, I was playing cards and drank far too much Sauternes. I overslept the next morning, and he set off without me. By the time I woke, he was sailing into that damned squall, convinced his yacht was invincible."

Court's voice broke on the last word, for they both knew just how very vulnerable the yacht had proven that day. It had capsized and sunk almost instantly, leaving the men aboard with no chance to save themselves.

"You couldn't have known the *Marguerite* would sink that

day," Vivi said softly, moving toward him, setting the box aside as she took his hands in hers. "No one knew that."

He took a deep breath and directed his gaze to the windows behind Vivi, unable to hold her stare. "But if I had been there at his side, I could have persuaded him to turn around before he reached the squall. I could have been the voice of reason he needed. And if I couldn't have done that, I'm a far stronger swimmer than Percy was. Perhaps I could have kept him from drowning. If I hadn't been so damned deep in my cups the night before, I would have been there for him when he needed me most. The guilt I feel over sleeping until noon that day has been haunting me ever since. Not only did I break my promise to the man I considered a brother, but I left him to die alone."

There. The ugly truth had finally left him, and he felt as if a weight had been lifted from his shoulders. Silence met his bitter confession, but Vivi's fingers were still laced through his. She hadn't rejected him yet.

"Court." She said his name so tenderly, mournfully, dragging his gaze back to hers.

And what he saw reflected in her eyes was neither anger nor disgust. It wasn't hatred or even grief. Instead, it was compassion.

"You shouldn't look at me like that," he rasped hoarsely. "I've been too bloody scared to tell you the full truth of that day for fear I'd lose you forever."

"So, instead, you left me."

"I had to, Vivi," he bit out. "I lived while he died, and then I broke my promise to him in a moment of weakness. I couldn't look at my damned reflection in the mirror, let alone you. But I couldn't stay away from you, either. I'm selfish and weak where you're concerned."

"I understand," she said, and then she wrapped her arms around him tightly, holding him close. "Nothing that happened was your fault, Court. And if you had been on the *Marguerite* with Percy that day, it's entirely possible that I would have lost you too. I couldn't have survived that. I'm glad you weren't aboard."

"Don't say that." He buried his face in her silken hair, inhaling deeply, love for her thundering through him. "I don't deserve to be here. I don't deserve to have you as my wife after everything I've done."

"Yes," she told him softly, warmly, the tenderness in her voice healing all the fissures inside him. "You do."

CHAPTER 11

$\mathcal{V}$ ivi was filled with a myriad of emotions as she took Court in her embrace. He clung to her, holding her against his tall, muscular frame as if she were his refuge. She slid her hands up and down his spine in calming, soothing motions, showing him without words all the pent-up feelings inside.

How she hated that he had been plagued by such guilt over Percy's death. She wished that he had confided in her before, but she understood for the first time, fully and completely, the magnitude of his grief and remorse over her brother's drowning. Not only had he broken his promise to Percy by making love to her in the boathouse that fateful night, he also believed himself somehow responsible for Percy's drowning.

He couldn't have been more wrong, but it was very like Court to have reckoned he might have done something to save his best friend or otherwise persuade him not to set sail that morning. He had always carried the burden of responsibility around with him—trying to please his cold and distant father, knowing he would one day become duke, attempting to earn his mother's love, although she was every bit as closed off as the duke had been.

"You're too good to me, Vivi," Court said, his voice sounding raw.

She wanted to tell him that she loved him, that she had for so many years, and that she had never been able to stop loving him, regardless of how hard she had tried. That loving him was as much a part of her as her marrow. But it felt too soon, too dangerous. Her heart was still recovering from the year he had been gone.

"I'm your wife," she offered instead. "It is my duty to be good to you."

He raised his head, staring down at her, looking so broken and beautiful that it ached just to look at him. "Is that all I am to you, then? A duty?"

"Of course not." She laid a hand on his cheek, the coarse bristles of his beard abrading her palm deliciously. "You are so much more than that."

His mouth came crashing down on hers, hot and demanding, a kiss that claimed as much as it gave. She welcomed it, welcomed him, opening for his questing tongue. Whether it was the height of their emotions or the sudden proximity between them, she couldn't say. But they were suddenly ravenous for each other.

He kissed her jaw, her throat, fingers flying over the buttons bisecting her bodice. She tugged at his neckcloth, sending it to the floor. The fastening on his waistcoat proved stubborn. Vivi made a low growl of frustration when she couldn't whisk it away as she wanted and tugged hard, buttons popping free. He shrugged it from his shoulders and tossed it aside before stripping her bodice off.

They stared at each other, breathless, lips dark from demanding kisses.

"Not here," Court said suddenly. "Not in this bloody room. It reminds me far too much of my father."

He took her hand and led her to the door adjoining their chambers. She didn't object, for there was nothing less seductive than the thought of the odious previous duke and the way he had mistreated Court. Her own room was blessedly empty, Nelson thankfully occupied with other tasks.

The door had scarcely closed before Court's lips were on hers again. Their mouths fused in a frantic mash, their desire fanning as high as the flames of their emotions. More cloth was pulled and torn away. More buttons and laces and tapes came undone.

Pins were spilling from her hair and raining over the Axminster, waves falling heavily over her shoulders and down her back. Vivi's corset loosened. Her bustle, skirts, and petticoat pooled at her feet in a puddle of silk and linen. With Court's help, she clawed his shirt from his broad chest and strong shoulders.

And then, her hands were everywhere. Coasting over his muscles, nails scraping down his flat, hard abdomen to the waistband of his trousers. She wanted them off. Wanted him naked. She told him with her tongue in his mouth, with her fumbling fingers working hard to open the fall. His cock was a tantalizing ridge straining against the placket. When she brushed over it in her efforts to undo buttons, he groaned into their kiss, the sound so potent, so helpless with desire, that she felt an answering surge of need between her legs. She palmed the tempting hardness, giving him a teasing caress that made him groan again and break the kiss.

"Damn it, Vivi," he said, his breathing harsh and ragged. "How am I supposed to resist you?"

The answer seemed simple enough.

"You're not," she told him, lips still tingling from the way he had possessed her mouth with those kisses.

Finally, she managed to slide another two buttons from their moorings, and the placket of his trousers opened, revealing the outline of his cock in his drawers. Impatient, she tugged his trousers down. He pulled the hooks on her corset from their corresponding eyes, and it fell to the floor atop her abandoned skirts. She was clad in nothing but her chemise and stockings, Court in his smalls.

He caught her waist in a gentle grasp and guided her backward toward her beckoning bed. "I want you more every damned day. I can't get enough of you."

"It is the same for me," she told him as the mattress abutted her legs and she sank down on it.

He dropped to his knees before her, dragging up the hem of her chemise to reveal her embroidered stockings and lace-edged garters. "Let me help you with these."

He took his time, caressing his way up her leg before slowly, tantalizingly, pulling the garter and stocking down and tossing it away. He took her other ankle in a masterful hold, his fingers massaging her lower calf muscle as they glided along. She thought she might combust from his touch through her stockings alone. But then he reached the second garter and rolled it and the stocking down her leg, and his knowing hands were moving on her bare skin, gliding higher and taking the hem of her chemise with them.

When he reached the tops of her thighs, she stopped him, her hands settling over his. "Do you still think that marrying me was a mistake?"

She didn't know where the question had come from, only that it had to be answered. The stakes of their lovemaking felt exponentially higher now that she understood how very torn he had been, the mantle of guilt he'd been wearing for the last year driving a wedge between them.

His fingertips dug incrementally into the give of her thighs, his gaze burning hotter than any fire as they met hers.

"I think marrying you was the best decision I ever made, Vivi. You're all I want. All I'll ever want. The only thing I regret was the haste and my lack of honor that night in the boathouse. If I could do it again, I would spare you the scandal and all the pain in the year that followed. I would marry you the proper way."

And those were the words she needed to hear.

Relief hit her, so vast that she would have gone toppling to the floor under the weight of it had he not been there to anchor her.

She released her hold on his hands. "Make love to me. I need you."

He lowered his head and kissed her knees, his hands dragging her chemise higher, until he reached her bottom and she wriggled to help him push the hem farther. She caught fistfuls of linen and dragged it over her head, sending it flying over Court's shoulder to the rest of their hastily discarded garments.

His traveling mouth and hands coaxed her legs apart, and she opened for him, desperate for his touch, his tongue. He gave her everything she wanted, stroking her first and then following his fingers with his lips.

He moaned against her as if he were a starving man in the midst of a feast. "You taste so sweet, and you're so wet for me."

She was in a shameless state, and she didn't care. Because he had given her a part of himself with his revelation, a reason to hope that he might one day love her the way she loved him.

"Please," she said, needing more.

He suckled her pearl, his fingers probing her entrance. In one slick glide, he was inside her, stretching her with that lone digit, probing deep. Bliss rushed through her, the breath fleeing her lungs. And then a second finger joined the first, pumping in and out of her, his tongue flicking over her clitoris in greedy, demanding swirls.

"Yes," she gasped out, already close.

So close.

Every lick and thrust sent her higher. Her physical need had joined with her deeper feelings for him. This wasn't just lovemaking. It was so much more than the slaking of needs and the claiming of each other's bodies. For Vivi, it was the beginning of a new chapter. The start of their future.

"Mmm," he groaned into her sex, rubbing his beard over her and increasing the pressure as he sucked, his fingers curling to find the place that never failed to make her fall apart.

The pleasure seized her with such force that she couldn't contain her cry. It echoed in the afternoon stillness, and anyone in the hall beyond would have heard it and known precisely what she and her husband were about. But she was too caught in the throes of her own bliss to care. Mindlessly, she rode out the lingering waves, rocking on his face and fingers. He stayed with her until the last spasm had calmed, and then he shucked his smalls and joined her on the bed, positioning them so that she was on her back with him atop her.

But no.

She had other plans.

Feeling bold, she urged Court to his back with a splayed hand on his chest. He did as she wanted, and she turned her attention to pleasuring him, dotting kisses over his shoulders, then lower. Down his abdomen where his muscles pulled taut and strong. To his hip bone.

"Vivi, what are you…"

She placed a kiss on the head of his length, her tongue flicking out to lap up the pearled bead of spend there.

"Ah, fuck…" he completed his trailing words with a groan.

"I want to make you come," she told him, wrapping her hand around the base of his glorious cock. "I want you to come in my mouth."

"Bloody hell," he bit out.

Which she understood to mean *yes, please*.

Vivi was eager to oblige. She took him into her mouth, teasing him with slow, steady licks. "Tell me what to do, how to pleasure you."

He raked a hand through his hair, head falling back on the pillow. "Everything you're doing. Use your mouth and hand and tongue. Lick and suck. Take me as deep as you can."

It was all the instruction she required. Vivi set herself to the task of making him come undone just as she had. She took his cock all the way to her throat, simultaneously stroking him as she knew he liked. He groaned, hips moving under her in time to the rhythm. The taste of him was musky and salty on her tongue, and she had to press her thighs together to stave off her own impatient need as she lavished attention on his cock.

"Enough," he growled from above, gently disengaging and guiding her so that she was atop him, his cock protruding against his stomach, glistening with her saliva. "I want to be inside you when I spend. I want to fill you with me."

His wicked words made her ache.

"Yes," she agreed breathlessly.

"Put me inside you, sweetheart," he commanded softly. "Ride me. Take what you want, what you need."

They had never made love in this position before, but Vivi couldn't deny that she savored the sense of power it gave her. Power over him, over pleasure, both shared and her own. She grasped him, guiding him to her entrance, letting out a low moan of pleasure as the tip of him probed her.

"Court," she moaned his name, beyond words, beyond anything other than feeling.

Pleasure and love were one, and she was happily burning in the flames.

"More," he said.

And she understood, because she needed that too. She sank down on him, taking his cock deep. The new angle was exquisite.

"Hell yes," he praised, his hands on her waist in a possessive hold she adored. "Now take me, sweetheart. Fuck me."

Tentatively, she moved, rising until he had almost slid free of her body and then sinking down hard to take him deep again. He helped set the pace, meeting her thrust for thrust, leaning up to take one of her nipples in his mouth. A flood of wetness rushed through her as she ground down on his cock and he sucked.

"You're perfect, Vivi," he said. "Made just for me."

She felt as if she were in that moment, her body so deliciously joined with his, the two of them seeking release together in unison. When he took her other nipple in his mouth, she rocked harder, impaling herself on his cock with greater determination. Once again, she was close. Everything inside her tightened to a beautiful, wild state of near-bliss.

His teeth grazed the peak of her breast, and his fingers found her swollen clitoris, rubbing persistent, delicious circles until it was too much. She cried out, coming hard, her release roaring through her as she continued to ride him, determined to make him lose control too.

"I'm going to come," he choked out, his words somehow heightening her body's reaction.

She wanted him to spend, to give her everything. Vivi clenched on his cock in response, her body knowing what it needed before her mind recognized it. Court stiffened beneath her, and she knew the hot spurt of his seed filling her up, the sensation sending a quivering series of miniature spasms through her.

Vivi collapsed atop him. He sifted a hand through her hair, stroking her back, his cock still throbbing inside her. Reverently, she kissed his chest just over his swiftly pounding heart, vowing to herself that, despite the looming house party and the anguish of the past, she would make that heart forever hers.

CHAPTER 12

"*Y*our Grace?"

"Not now," Vivi muttered, waving a hand in the direction of Nelson's voice, eyes still firmly closed.

After a night spent alternately lovemaking and sleeping with her husband—with the emphasis on lovemaking—she was thoroughly exhausted. And she had no wish to open her eyes to the impossibly bright light seeping through her eyelids just now.

"Close the curtains," she added. "It's far too bright in here."

"Your Grace, the curtains *are* closed," Nelson said, her voice sounding oddly strained.

And that was when it occurred to Vivi with sudden, embarrassing clarity, the reason for her lady's maid's discomfort. Court was still in her bed. He had been too tired to return to his chamber the night before, and she had welcomed the comfort of his presence, not thoroughly considering the morning consequences.

Dear heavens, was he covered?

Forcing her eyes open, Vivi sat up, holding the bedclothes over her naked breasts, only to find that her rumpled bed was empty, no husband to be found. She frowned as she took in Nelson next, standing halfway across the room, looking hesitant and distressed all at once. That was also when she discovered that her lady's maid was correct. The curtains were indeed closed. The sun pouring through the edges of them had been the source of the intrusion of light.

"It's exceedingly bright for seven o'clock in the morning," she observed, frowning.

"That is because it is no longer morning, Your Grace," Nelson informed her. "Forgive me for waking you, but—"

"No longer morning?" Vivi interrupted. "What in heaven's name do you mean?"

It couldn't be. Vivi woke at half past six each morning as a matter of habit, always long awake before Nelson arrived at one quarter past seven. She never overslept.

"Yes, Your Grace, it is half past one in the afternoon," Nelson said. "And the guests have begun arriving, or else I wouldn't have deigned to intrude on your slumber. I hope you don't mind."

"Guests? Half past one?" Alarm seized her. "They're here? Which guests? Oh dear heavens, Nelson. This is an utter disaster."

"Lady Charity Manners has arrived with her aunt, Lady Louise Manners. Miss Madeline Chartrand with her sister, Miss Lucy Chartrand, have come from the train station, and there is also Lady Edith Smythe and the Marchioness of Featherstone," Nelson told her.

All her dearest friends. That was hardly a concern. One name, however, decidedly was.

She pressed the back of her hand to her forehead, dismay chasing the sleepiness from her. "Not Lady Featherstone."

The idyll she had shared with Court the day before had decidedly come to a jarring end.

"The marchioness is naturally accompanying her daughter," Nelson said, having no notion of how much Vivi feared the woman's sharp tongue and penchant for spreading gossip.

"It is merely that I wished to greet the marchioness upon her arrival," Vivi explained tactfully.

So that the dragon wouldn't find fault in her as a hostess and deny Lady Edith the ability to join the Lady's Suffrage Society.

"His Grace is attending the guests in your absence," Nelson said in a tone of calm reassurance. "I believe he was making arrangements with Mrs. Porritt for Lady Featherstone and her daughter."

That was hardly comforting to Vivi. Court was greeting her guests while she had been sleeping after they'd made love all night long. What a scandalous wretch she was. Surely everyone would wonder at the reason for her lack of appearance, to say nothing for the reason behind Court's presence.

As far as Society knew, Court was still traveling the world, leaving her behind. And now he was here, donning the role of dutiful husband. A role he had played quite excellently not just the past fortnight but particularly the night before, and the state of her bed and her aching body provided ample testament to that.

Heat stole over her cheeks in remembrance. Did Nelson know what had happened? Could she tell? Vivi looked down at herself and had to admit that it would be impossible for her lady's maid not to suspect. How embarrassing.

"Why did no one wake me?" she demanded to know. "Quarter past seven, Nelson. It is our standing arrangement."

Now, it was the domestic's turn for her cheeks to go red. She diverted her gaze, busying herself with preparing Vivi's toilette. "I'm afraid I did arrive, Your Grace. However, His Grace bid me to return later. I didn't wish to displease him."

Court had sent her lady's maid away. That confirmed it. Nelson *did* know that he had spent the night in her bed. Not that it was wrong, nor should she be ashamed. He was her husband, after all. However, she had never navigated such a delicate situation before, Court having left the day after their wedding, after a wedding night that had been decidedly chaste. Each night since his return, he had been careful to leave her bed some time before dawn.

"Of course," she muttered. "Forgive me, Nelson. It is merely that I am at sixes and sevens. I don't oversleep, nor do I neglect my duties as a hostess."

Lady Featherstone would carry this gossip straight back to London. Of that, she was certain. And Vivi didn't care about being fodder for wagging tongues quite so much as she feared the effect it might have on the Lady's Suffrage Society She would never dream of doing anything to hinder their cause.

"His Grace is doing splendidly," Nelson told her. "Will it be the cream silk afternoon gown?"

It was the dress she had chosen previously for greeting her guests. But now that Court had returned and they had spent the last two weeks as husband and wife, the cream dress felt far too demure.

"Perhaps the ice-blue silk instead," she said, for it matched her eyes.

The train was trimmed with feathers, and the underskirt was accented with damask and blonde lace. Although the décolletage was demure and buttoned to the neck, the bold-ness of the gown made her feel lush and alluring. She had commissioned it on a whim from a dressmaker favored by Lady Jo Danvers, but she had only worn it on one previous occasion.

"Of course, Your Grace," Nelson said with politic ease, whisking away the cream silk gown.

While her lady's maid disappeared into the dressing room, Vivi bit her lip, looking down at her dishabille, covered only with the bedclothes. She always slept in a night rail. But Court had kept her too busy to care. Now, it would seem she was stranded in her bed, with no means of answering her modesty.

Nelson returned bearing a dressing gown and a smile, bustling to Vivi's side. "Your dressing gown, Your Grace."

Gratitude swept over her. She might have known that the ever-proficient lady's maid would know precisely what to do in such a circumstance. Nelson held out the robe for her to don. Hastily, Vivi slipped from the bed, stuffing her arms into the sleeves.

"Thank you, Nelson." She wrapped the twain ends around herself and fastened the belt. "I must admit that I find myself woefully inadequately prepared for a house party and a husband both."

"You are an excellent hostess, Your Grace," Nelson told her, ushering her toward the dressing room. "And you are undeniably a credit to His Grace as well."

Vivi wanted to ask her lady's maid how she could be so certain about the latter when it had only been a fortnight since her husband's return. She may have been a wife for over a year, but she had only felt like one for a sum of fourteen days. Everything was painfully, frighteningly new, especially the depth of her love for him, stronger than ever.

"You are a dear heart," she said instead.

"Never fret about your guests," Nelson added as she laid out a freshly laundered chemise and drawers. "The duke has them all quite wound around his finger like a thread."

And, Vivi thought as she began to dress, much like herself as well.

~

As he politely listened to the Marchioness of Featherstone droning on about the merits of ladies staying close to home and hearth, Court thought that if he was expected to spend the next two weeks with such a wrong-headed bag of wind, he might be tempted to throw her from a window just to see if she would take flight in the manner of a kite. But he could endure, he admonished himself sternly. He *would* endure. All for the sake of his wife, who was currently still abed upstairs after he had spent the night making love to her as often as his cock had allowed.

As it had happened, his cock was an indisputably randy prick.

Ah, if only the marchioness knew the filth that was invading his mind and that the polite excuse he'd given for Vivi's absence was utter claptrap. Or that mere hours before, when dawn had been cresting over the sleepy Yorkshire landscape, his tongue had been deep inside his wife's cunny yet again and she'd been eager and so very wet, making the most deliciously wicked sounds.

The dragon would likely snort her *Partridge à la Clarence* out her haughty nose at the vaguest hint of such untoward behavior.

He hid his smile in his glass of wine, feigning interest in Lady Featherstone's endless conversation. Although he was inordinately proud of the fact that he had so thoroughly sated his wife that she had slept past noon for the first time in her life, he was beginning to doubt the wisdom of joining her houseguests for luncheon.

Initially, he had been grateful for the distraction after the heaviness of his revelations to Vivi the day before and their incredible night together. His heart was wound tighter than a watch spring, and he was desperate to make the last confession to her he hoped he ever needed to—that being his love for her. He was also terrified to tell her, not entirely knowing what to expect. Neither of them had spoken of finer emotions during their sensual idyll. The night had been about pleasure and reunion, about making amends for all the hurt and pain that had come between them.

"I know you shall be an improving influence upon Her Grace," Lady Featherstone told him with an ominous air, as if her words were more threat than prediction.

And although she sipped her soup with perfect aplomb and the exquisite manners to which she had undoubtedly been born, the marchioness somehow managed to drip a tiny chunk of meat directly on the black pleated silk adorning her bodice. There it remained, like a jaunty little salute.

He could only think that even the partridge found Lady Featherstone insufferable.

Why the devil had Vivi invited such a paragon of hypo-critical virtue? If there was a good reason, he couldn't, for the life of him, think of one in this moment.

"You are most kind," he managed, forcing a smile. "How-ever, I am reasonably certain that it is Her Grace who shall be the improving influence upon myself."

"I wholeheartedly agree," said Lady Charity Manners from down the table. "I fear you have confused matters, Lady Featherstone. You see, His Grace has been traveling abroad for the last year, and it is plain to see that Her Grace has rung the bell to call him home. I daresay a bit of domesticity is just what he needs."

Another of Vivi's circle that had formed in his absence, Lady Charity was brash and audacious. She had been goading Lady Featherstone since their arrival, and he couldn't deny that he admired the younger lady's ability to hold her own against the dowager. Lesser women would have already waved the white flag of surrender beneath Lady Featherstone's censorious glare and withering setdowns.

Even so, his masculine pride winced at her suggesting Vivi had rung a bell and he had bounded home like a mongrel being called to dinner.

"Of course it is domesticity that every gently bred man requires," Lady Featherstone snapped before Court could speak. "However, a gentleman also requires his own sphere, in which a good wife never must intrude. It is the husband's prerogative to do as he must, and it is the duty of the wife to obey her husband in all things. Is that not so, dear daughter?"

She turned her question and her sharp gaze upon Lady Edith, who had the misfortune to be seated at Lady Featherstone's side, in addition to the misfortune of having been born the detestably opinionated woman's daughter.

"Of course, Mother," Lady Edith said dutifully, offering a wan smile.

She was painfully shy, with brilliant red hair and a pair of spectacles perched on her freckled nose. Court had met Lady Edith and her mother in passing at various Society gatherings over the years. And it rather saddened him to see that, although it had been some time since he'd last crossed paths with the pair, Lady Edith remained just as firmly under her mother's thumb as ever. Hardly surprising, he supposed. The marchioness's personality was sharp as a blade. Lady Edith would likely remain unwed for life.

"Perhaps a good wife ought to intrude in some instances," he suggested lightly, nettled by Lady Featherstone, despite the amusing addition to her bodice. "I am certain that most gentlemen appreciate the opinions and companionship of their wives both."

"Opinions?" the marchioness scoffed, and this time, another small sliver of partridge went sailing from her mouth to the snowy white table linen, landing perilously near to the epergne. "It is not a lady's place to have any opinions at all."

"None?" Lady Clementine asked, a note of outrage in her voice.

"Perhaps one," suggested Lady Edith quietly.

Meekly.

The poor chit.

Someone had to rescue her from her mother. That much was apparent.

"Perhaps it is done differently here in England," Miss Lucy Chartrand said archly. "But in America, a woman is entitled to as many opinions as she likes."

"And being an American, no doubt you have many," Lady Featherstone said sourly.

"I am reasonably certain that all women harbor opinions, be they in America or England," added Miss Madeline Chartrand pointedly.

The sisters hailed from a hideously wealthy family that was essentially New York City royalty. It was apparent that the eldest daughters were making inroads in the English aristocracy. Likely, their parents were eager for them to make advantageous matches. It wouldn't be the first time that a wealthy American family secured a lord for its daughter, nor, he knew, would it be the last.

"It is not the existence of opinions that matters, Miss Chartrand," Lady Featherstone announced loftily. "Rather, it is the airing of them."

Ah, hell. Where was more wine when he needed it? His glass was empty. He signaled to a footman. For that matter, where were some fellow men when he needed them? He'd give his left ballock to be away from this hideous spectacle of a luncheon, hidden away somewhere playing billiards or riding or shooting. Anything. Anything at all that would take him away from Lady Featherstone.

At that moment, he was saved by the appearance of his wife. Wearing a pale-blue gown that had him longing to carry her back to bed, tear it off her, and make love to her again, she was astonishingly lovely. She moved with confidence and poise, and had he not been seated, he likely would have fallen on his arse.

For here, before him, was a Vivi he had never previously seen.

It was the Vivi she had become without him. Bold, brave, commanding, elegant, and more beautiful than ever. Pride stirred inside him.

He stood with such haste, he nearly knocked his chair over in his eagerness to escort her to the table. "Duchess."

Court presented her with a courtly bow and then offered her his arm.

She accepted it, smiling brightly at the gathered assemblage—the ladies who were a mere hint of the guests that were to come. "I am so pleased that you all could join us for the next fortnight," she announced to the table at large.

He hoped to God she wasn't including Lady Featherstone in that statement. Court would speak to her about the matter of her ladyship insulting her and the rest of the ladies present later. Instead, he escorted her to the place setting which he'd had ordered laid for her, at his side, and pulled out her chair.

As she seated herself, the scent of her wafted up to him, teasing his senses, making his cock twitch. The next fortnight—continuing to woo his wife with an audience of houseguests—was going to be a challenge. Of that, he was certain. But Vivi was worth it, and they'd already spent far too much time apart. He would gladly endure all the Lady Featherstones of the world if it meant he could win his wife's love and trust. He owed it to Vivi—and Percy—to make her happy.

CHAPTER 13

*V*ivi was already exhausted, and many more houseguests were still yet to arrive. Lady Featherstone was being every bit as dreadful as Vivi had feared she would be. Luncheon had been something of a disaster, despite the pleasant attempts of her friends to redirect conversation from the marchioness. Vivi had been incredibly aware of her husband's presence at her side for the duration, and she couldn't deny how right it felt to have him there. To share not just her bed with him, but every other aspect of her life.

He had been the piece of herself that had been missing. And yet, she remained torn between her love for him and her fears that one day, he might find another reason to leave her or that he would never return her love, no matter how hard she tried to earn his heart.

When the meal had been completed, the tension in the room had been thick enough to cut with a knife, and Vivi had been eager for an excuse to escape. She had ventured to the gardens to make certain the final chessboard had been painted on the north lawn.

And now she was lingering in the rosebushes, savoring a moment of peace amidst the mayhem, wondering for the hundredth time why she had decided to host this house party after all. Perhaps it had been a spectacularly bad idea. Also hoping she wouldn't regret her decision to let Court back into her life and into her bed.

For he had never been gone from her heart. And now that he had come back to her, with his charm and determination to woo her and the sincere explanations she had so desperately needed to help her understand him, her husband had entrenched himself all the more firmly.

Running her finger along one of the rosebuds, its petals still tightly closed, she sighed heavily before doing something that had become a comforting habit in the wake of Percy's death—talking to her beloved brother.

"Oh, Percy," she murmured softly. "I love him. I always have since I was but a foolish girl of fourteen with no true notion of what love was, only that I felt it deep in my heart whenever I was with him. But I'm terrified he will hurt me again."

There it was, the truth she hadn't dared allow herself to linger upon for too long during the past two weeks. She understood Court's reasons for leaving, even if she didn't agree with his decision. Grief over Percy's death had changed her as well. In those early days, she had been broken inside, too wounded to make sense of much of anything. But then Court had left her when she had needed him. In the span of a few short weeks, both of the men she loved the most had left her. And although she understood how conflicted Court must have been, given his promise to Percy, she couldn't shake the fear that she would wake up one morning to the same curt stranger who had left her that day without an explanation.

If he walked away from her a second time, she wasn't sure she would survive the pain.

Tears burned her eyes, threatening to spill. She missed her brother so much. Missed his smile, his laughter, his warm embraces. Missed the way he had teased her. Missed riding with him, the way he had listened to her, championed her always.

But then, hadn't Court done that as well? Looking back on her life, it seemed to her now that it had always been the three of them. Until it had only been the two of them. Not even the strong bonds she shared with her parents had ever compared.

She sniffed, fighting the sorrow as she whispered, "You were the best brother I could have asked for, Percy. I'll miss you always."

What would have happened if he had not drowned in the Bristol Channel that day? If the *Marguerite* had not sunk in that terrible squall? If he had never gone aboard his yacht, never made the trip to Devon? She had asked herself those questions many times, and there existed no answers which weren't painful.

Vivi liked to think Percy would have understood just how much she loved Court. That he would have been happy the two of them had married, despite the promise he'd forced Court to make. But she would never truly know. Her brother was forever lost to her. All that remained was the future, if she was daring enough to entrust herself to it.

The sweet warbling of a nearby bird reached Vivi then, bringing her back from the murky depths of the past just as a footfall on the gravel path sent it winging away. She turned to find Court approaching her, dashing as ever, a tender smile on his lips that was for her alone.

"I thought I might find you here," he said.

"You were looking for me?" she asked, surprised.

He had told her his intention to meet with the land steward whilst she worked out the remaining details of the house party. She hadn't expected to see him again so soon after luncheon, whilst the guests settled into their private apartments. And yet, it was fitting that he was here, that he had found her in a moment so profound.

Just when she needed him most.

Court stopped before her, suddenly solemn. "I've been looking for you always, Vivi. Everywhere."

Those felt like the only words she needed him to say, so magnificent and bursting with promise. The only words she ever wished to hear again, save three precious ones that may never be hers.

The tears that had yet to fall remained, threatening to spill. "I've been right here, waiting for you."

"I know you have." Gently, he brushed a tendril of hair from her cheek. "You have been steadfast and true, and a man could not ask for a better wife than you."

"I know I'm not the wife you wanted," she said.

"You are the only wife I wanted, and the one I thought I could never have," he countered softly. "I love you, Vivi."

The words she had longed to hear.

Those beautiful, stunning words coming from the heart of the man she had loved for twelve long and painful years to no avail. She swayed, so affected by the implications of it all that she might have fallen had Court not been there to slide a possessive arm around her waist and anchor her to him.

The tears were falling, blurring her vision. She blinked frantically to dash them away so that she could see his beloved face without hindrance as she clutched his shoulders, holding him to her, lest he tried to pull away. No, she was not letting go of him now. Nor ever again.

"You...love...me," she repeated haltingly, as if she spoke a strange, new foreign language.

Because that was how it felt, this sudden knowledge that Court loved her.

He nodded, looking solemn and so beautifully handsome, and so different from the dashing young clean-shaven gentleman she had met as a girl. He had matured, growing into his form, all lean muscle and courtly grace with a masculinity that was somehow a hundredfold more potent than it had been before.

"Did you not know it?" he asked.

She stroked his jaw, loving the abrasion of his beard on her tender skin. Loving *him*. "I was too afraid to hope. I've loved you for so long. When I was a girl and you were a handsome young man come to Edmonds House for the first time. When I was a debutante and you danced with me at the Needham ball. When you came to me, broken and grief-stricken over Percy's death. When you made love to me in the boathouse, when you married me. Even when you were far from me, I never stopped loving you. I've known it in my heart, in my soul. What I never knew was that you loved me too."

"My God, Vivi." His voice was raw, his countenance a reflection of his emotions—so much naked love writ across the handsome angles and planes. "I had no notion. I never dreamed you felt the same for me."

"Nor did you ask," she pointed out wryly.

But then, she had not asked him either.

"You know the reason I could not," he said quietly.

And they were back to Percy again. To the man they had both loved as brother, as friend. To the broken promise. To the death of him and their world as they had known it.

"I speak to him sometimes," she said. "To Percy. I was speaking to him just now, when you found me. And then I heard a bird singing, and there you were. It may be silliness on my part, but I can't help but feel he was here with me, just for a moment. He loved us both, Court. I cannot think he would wish for us to be miserable apart."

"We have honored him every way we could," Court agreed. "I'd like to believe that he would be happy for us. That he would want our future to be filled with love and joy and each other."

Another bird flew overhead, trilling a song in its wake.

"That's all I have ever wanted for myself, is to be your wife," she said, still stroking his beard, emotion welling inside her. "To love you. To be loved by you."

He turned his head and kissed her palm reverently. "The time has come to stop living for the past and to live instead in the future we create together."

"Yes." She smiled, swallowing against another onslaught of tears. "I want that more than you'll ever know."

"I want it too, just as I want you, Vivi. In my life, by my side, in my bed. I want a family with you. Hell, I even want to host this house party with you, despite the harridan you invited for reasons that shall forever mystify me."

A giggle escaped her. "Keep your voice down, or Lady Featherstone shall hear you. And I told you, it is for the good of the cause. The more supporters of the Lady's Suffrage Society that we can find, the better we shall be for it, and the greater our chance of affecting change."

He smiled down at her. "One thing is for certain. The next fortnight will be deuced interesting. But I wouldn't have it any other way if it means I can share it with you."

"I feel the same." She caught her lip in her teeth then, a wicked idea coming over her. "Speaking of our guests, we do have a bit of time before the next train arrives."

"Say no more." He kissed her swiftly. "I fear that there is a matter of great import that needs our attention in your bedroom." He paused, and then, as if he could not resist, kissed her again before continuing, "Immediately."

"How right you are. We should make haste." She looped her arm through his, and together, they followed the path through the rose garden with the sun shining down on them and the birds singing above.

EPILOGUE

TWO WEEKS LATER

"*I* wasn't wrong, was I?"

Vivi was seated at the mirror in her bedroom, removing her earrings, as Court approached her, looking sinfully handsome in his evening finery. She took a moment to admire her husband's dashing form before answering.

"Wrong about what, darling?" The diamond-and-pearl earrings he had brought her from New York City were returned neatly to their case as she watched him.

He had gifted them to her earlier that evening before the house party's final ball, along with the matching necklace that was still clasped at her throat. Court reached her and settled warm hands atop shoulders revealed by the cut of her beaded silk evening gown, the connection sending a frisson of desire through her. Vivi couldn't control her response to her husband; each day that passed only served to draw them closer and make her want him more.

"That the fortnight would be deuced interesting," he said, bending down to deliver a kiss to her nape.

She couldn't suppress her hum of pure pleasure at the sensation of his sensual lips caressing her skin.

"More interesting than either of us could have ever supposed," she agreed. "I daresay our house party will be the talk of Society for some time to come."

He feathered openmouthed kisses along her neck, working his way to her ear, and she shivered with delight.

"Do you suppose that love and happiness are catching?" he asked, his lips grazing the shell of her ear as he spoke.

"One must wonder after everything that has transpired over the last two weeks," she agreed, reaching back to thread her fingers through Court's thick, dark hair.

All five of her closest friends had managed to find themselves engaged by the house party's conclusion. If anyone would have told Vivi a mere two weeks ago, she wouldn't have believed it. But there was something undeniably romantic in the air at Sherborne Manor. Their little coterie was expanding to include the men who loved them, and she couldn't be more pleased, particularly since it meant that support for the Lady's Suffrage Society was effectively doubling.

Court's lips found the sensitive hollow behind her ear.

"You told me Lady Clementine was the matchmaker, but I begin to wonder," he murmured, kissing down her throat now. "You are, after all, the architect of this gathering. Did you plan it?"

She tilted her head back, giving him more access, still sifting her fingers through his hair. "I merely invited gentlemen I felt would be amenable to our cause and best positioned to help us. Dukes were most wanted, of course. There is nothing so influential as a duke."

He stopped at the place where her neck and shoulder met, delivering a nip that made liquid heat pool between her thighs. "Is that all we dukes are adept at, being influential?"

As he finished the question, he moved his left hand with wicked intent, sliding it down her accommodating bodice and inside her corset to cup her breast. Her nipple tightened in instant gratitude, and she arched her back.

"I cannot speak for all dukes," she managed breathlessly, "but the duke I love is also incredibly talented with his hands, his lips, and his tongue."

He bit her shoulder, slowly caressing her nipple. "You disappoint me. You've forgotten what I'm most proficient at."

She hadn't, of course. But she certainly did enjoy teasing him. She and Court had fallen into a blissful state, the past not forgotten but where it belonged—behind them. Letting go of pain and hurt had left them both free to revel in their love and in each other. Percy would always be a part of them, but some promises, they had discovered, were meant to be broken.

"What is it you're most proficient at, dearest husband?" she asked coquettishly, watching the erotic picture they presented in the mirror, Court's big hand down her bodice and his mouth devouring her bare skin.

He rubbed his beard lightly against her cheek, and heaven help her, but she was thinking of how wonderful that beard felt on her sex and her inner thighs. "If you don't recall, I'll just have to show you."

Desire pulsed through her. "Please do, my duke."

"Your duke," he repeated, his voice low and deep and sultry. "I like the sound of that."

She turned toward him, so close their noses brushed. "Forever my duke."

And then she kissed him, and her duke proceeded to fulfill his promise of showing her just where his greatest talent of all lay—in loving her.

∾

THANK you for reading *Forever Her Duke*. I hope you loved Vivi and Court's second chance romance and that, like me, you're looking forward to a return to the beloved world of my Notorious Ladies of London. As the house party unfolds, reader favorites and a cast of new bold, independent ladies will collide. Read on for an excerpt from Clementine's happily ever after, *Forever Her Marquess*. I hope you'll adore this thoroughly revised version of her and Dorset's story.

Please stay in touch! The only way to be sure you'll know what's next from me is to sign up for my newsletter here: http://eepurl.com/dyJSar. Please join my reader group for early excerpts, cover reveals, and more here. And if you're in the mood to chat all things steamy historical romance and read a different book each month, join my book club, Dukes Do It Hotter right here: https://www.facebook.com/groups/hotdukes because we're having a whole lot of fun! Now, on to that sneak peek…

Chapter One

She was in the wrong bedroom.

Clementine realized her error the moment she swept into the chamber, breathless and abuzz with anticipation of the prank she intended to play on her friend, Lady Charity Manners. It was the scent that alerted her first.

Musky and manly with a decisive edge of citrus and a note of something richer. It was an enticing scent, she couldn't lie. The sort of scent that made her wonder to whom it belonged.

And then it was the personal items neatly laid out on a nearby dresser, including a leather case which had been left open to reveal a brush, a razor, and a small tin of shaving soap. Beside that, a box of cigars and some matches. These were the trappings of men and most certainly not the delicate, elegant brushes and pots to be expected in the toilette of a lady.

"Oh dear," she muttered to herself.

She had, quite clearly, managed to land herself in a gentleman's chamber. And the footsteps beyond in the hall, coupled with the deep, masculine voices, told her that it was entirely possible the gentleman in question was about to return.

Frantically, Clementine searched for a means of escape as the voices in the hall came nearer. But there was no other means of exit save the door she had just entered.

As a self-professed matchmaker, Clementine knew better than anyone just how damning it could be to find one's self unexpectedly alone in the wrong room with someone. Particularly when she had no notion of who that someone was.

Where could she go? How could she hide? A glance at the imposing high tester nestled against the far wall proved hiding beneath it an unreliable option. She would never manage to squeeze herself, bustle and all, under the frame. Her gaze lit on the voluminous curtains bracketing the window that overlooked the Sherborne Manor park.

Perhaps she could hide herself behind one half of the drapery.

Frantic, she hastened across the Axminster before sliding behind the curtain. She scarcely had a moment to arrange the window dressing around her and attempt to flatten her skirts before the door to the bedroom swung open.

"...a game of billiards later, old chap."

Her breath caught in her throat at the voice, for she knew exactly to whom it belonged.

And the Marquess of Dorset despised her.

The feeling was mutual.

It all stemmed, she suspected, from her matchmaking

attempts between Lady Anna Harcastle and the Marquess of Huntly. Attempts which had proven successful when Lady Anna and Huntly had fallen desperately in love and married. How was Clementine to have known that Dorset had possessed a secret *tendre* for Lady Anna himself?

She closed her eyes tightly, wondering why of all the rooms she might have inadvertently entered by mistake, she should have found *his*.

Because that was the rotten nature of the luck she had. Which was to say, she had none at all. It would have been a fate far better to have found herself accidentally inside Lady Featherstone's chamber, and the dowager marchioness was a vicious-tongued gossip everyone sought to avoid at all costs.

The click of the door closing was followed by footfalls on the carpet.

She held her breath.

"Since when do curtains have feet?" he drawled.

Oh, blast. Her heart plummeted. The dratted window covering wasn't long enough, and he had spied her. Perhaps if she said nothing, he would be a gentleman, understand she'd entered the wrong room, and go away so that she might escape in peace.

Any hope of that was dashed when the curtain was whisked aside, and she was presented with the sight of the Marquess of Dorset hovering over her, too tall and vexingly handsome, his vibrant, green eyes narrowing when he recognized her.

"You," he growled, his lip curling into a sneer.

"My lord," she began, only to be interrupted.

"What the devil are you doing in my room, Lady Clementine?" the marquess demanded.

She cleared her throat, giving him her most winning smile in the hopes it might dim some of his ire. "I have a perfectly good explanation."

His jaw tensed. "If you're intending to cause more trouble, be warned, madam. I'll not suffer your machinations."

His disdain for her was palpable. He had made his dislike for her known on several occasions at Society events. However, he had never been so brutally earnest.

"I was seeking Lady Charity's chamber," she explained. "I intended to give her a fright when she entered. However, I must have made a mistake, because this is not her room."

"It is mine."

"I can see that now," she said weakly, keenly aware of the window at her back and his big body between herself and the door. "I apologize for the inconvenience."

"You expect me to believe you innocently wandered into the wrong room?"

"Yes."

"*You?* The lady notorious for all her matchmaking escapades, for catching couples in compromising positions, had no notion of which room she was entering?"

She smiled encouragingly. "Yes."

"Ha!" He barked out a vicious, bitter burst of laughter so sudden and loud it caused her to flinch. "You must think me the world's greatest idiot."

Her mouth moved, unable to form sentences for a moment. In truth, she did think him an idiot, but for a different reason entirely.

"Perhaps not the world's greatest," she allowed, unable to hold her tongue.

The Marquess of Dorset simply had that effect upon her. He was a bitter rake who was handsome and knew it too well. Who had left a trail of broken hearts in his dazzlingly elegant wake. He was the sort of man a lady of intellect never dared trust.

"Do you know what I ought to do, Lady Clementine?" he asked, stroking his jaw idly, as if he had all the time in the world to corner her here against the window of his bedroom.

"Yes," she said tartly. "You ought to step aside so that I may go."

"Not yet, I don't think," Dorset said smoothly.

She considered a means of escape, but he was standing so close, and she feared that movement in any direction would lead to either her bringing down the drapes or brushing against him.

"Dorset," she protested pointedly. "Surely you realize that my lingering here is a risk neither of us should dare to take."

"Hmm," was all he said, a troubling glint entering his eye. "Why not, Lady Clementine?"

"You know precisely why."

"What if I don't? Explain it to me, if you please."

Her panic was rising. The longer she remained trapped in his room with him, the greater the danger of discovery.

She took a step to the right, her bustle brushing along the windowpane and catching on something. Dorset took a step as well, his countenance bordering on fiendish.

He was enjoying her entrapment, she realized. Enjoying her discomfiture.

"My lord," she tried again, seeking mercy and reason, two traits which he apparently lacked.

Dorset smiled, and she couldn't deny the effect it had on her. "Enlighten me. I'll wait."

Her cheeks were vexingly hot. If she'd been carrying a fan, she would have put it to excellent use. And perhaps also used it to poke him soundly in the eye.

"If I am seen leaving your room by any of our fellow guests, scandal will be unavoidable," she gritted through clenched teeth. "I haven't come to this house party to set tongues wagging or find myself entrapped in a marriage of convenience."

"Do you imagine any of your past victims sought to be trapped?" he asked sharply.

Victims? Why, he made it sound as if she were a murderer stalking the streets in the darkest night, claiming souls.

"I haven't any victims," she countered coldly. "Now if you please, move so that I may pass and remove myself from this dreadful situation."

"Always interesting when the spider gets caught in her own web," he said.

And Clementine quite lost her patience.

"Blast it, Dorset," she blurted, "are you a madman?"

He gave her a speculative look. "In addition to being an idiot, you mean?"

He was *definitely* a madman.

Vivi had invited a lunatic to her country house party, and now Clementine was trapped with him.

She tried sweeping to the right, but her bustle remained caught. The sound of tearing echoed in the quiet of the room.

"Oh good heavens," she cried, truly in distress now, for she was wearing one of her favorite afternoon gowns, and there was only one thing worse than being discovered alone with the Marquess of Dorset in his bedroom, and that was being discovered alone with him whilst her gown bore a giant tear in the silk skirts.

Everyone would think something terribly unseemly had occurred.

"I do believe you've torn a hole in your gown," Dorset observed calmly. "You should have taken greater care."

"How was I to have taken greater care, you lummox?" Clementine pushed at his insufferably broad shoulders, but the bounder refused to budge. "This is all your fault. You entrapped me here and wouldn't allow me to go."

"You entrapped yourself, Lady Clementine." He frowned

down at her, craning his neck, still unmoving despite her efforts. "Turn, if you please. Allow me to see the damage done."

She didn't want him to inspect her ruined gown. Didn't want his assistance. Most assuredly didn't want his proximity. The scent she had detected upon first entering the bedroom was more pronounced now—coming from *him*. And it was disturbingly pleasant, despite the distinctly irritating source.

"Kindly move away so that I can see for myself," she ordered him.

He made a *tsk* sound, as if he were warning a naughty child. "Have you eyes in the back of your head?"

"No, but I've a neck that turns."

"I'm only trying to help you."

They glared at each other.

The sound of more voices in the hall reached her. Clementine huffed a sigh, surrendering.

"Very well," she muttered. "If you must."

She turned to the sound of more ripping silk.

"It would seem your gown is still stuck on the tieback," he said.

"Obviously," she ground out. "Why did you not tell me so before I turned?"

She knew the answer, of course. It was because he was a devious rogue.

He leaned nearer, the press of his large body against hers inevitable as he struggled to pull her silk from the gilt hook upon which it had been helplessly snagged. And curse him, but his nearness wasn't entirely despicable.

She was *moved*, something inside her tightening, growing acutely aware of him in a new and dangerous way.

Clementine held her breath and averted her gaze out the window. And that was when she saw the dragon marchioness, Lady Featherstone, walking on the path below with her daughter, Lady Edith. Clementine gasped, horror clawing at her. She could not afford to be seen in the Marquess of Dorset's bedroom window. Not by anyone, but most especially not by the dowager.

Mindlessly, she threw herself at the marquess.

There was another great rending of fabric, and then the two of them toppled as one to the Axminster.

Want more? Get *Forever Her Marquess* now.

DON'T MISS SCARLETT'S OTHER ROMANCES!

Complete Book List
HISTORICAL ROMANCE

Heart's Temptation
A Mad Passion (Book One)
Rebel Love (Book Two)
Reckless Need (Book Three)
Sweet Scandal (Book Four)
Restless Rake (Book Five)
Darling Duke (Book Six)
The Night Before Scandal (Book Seven)

Wicked Husbands
Her Errant Earl (Book One)
Her Lovestruck Lord (Book Two)
Her Reformed Rake (Book Three)
Her Deceptive Duke (Book Four)
Her Missing Marquess (Book Five)
Her Virtuous Viscount (Book Six)

League of Dukes
Nobody's Duke (Book One)
Heartless Duke (Book Two)
Dangerous Duke (Book Three)
Shameless Duke (Book Four)
Scandalous Duke (Book Five)
Fearless Duke (Book Six)

Notorious Ladies of London
Lady Ruthless (Book One)
Lady Wallflower (Book Two)
Lady Reckless (Book Three)
Lady Wicked (Book Four)
Lady Lawless (Book Five)
Lady Brazen (Book 6)

Unexpected Lords
The Detective Duke (Book One)
The Playboy Peer (Book Two)
The Millionaire Marquess (Book Three)
The Goodbye Governess (Book Four)

Dukes Most Wanted
Forever Her Duke (Book One)
Forever Her Marquess (Book Two)

The Wicked Winters
Wicked in Winter (Book One)
Wedded in Winter (Book Two)
Wanton in Winter (Book Three)
Wishes in Winter (Book 3.5)
Willful in Winter (Book Four)
Wagered in Winter (Book Five)
Wild in Winter (Book Six)

Wooed in Winter (Book Seven)
Winter's Wallflower (Book Eight)
Winter's Woman (Book Nine)
Winter's Whispers (Book Ten)
Winter's Waltz (Book Eleven)
Winter's Widow (Book Twelve)
Winter's Warrior (Book Thirteen)
A Merry Wicked Winter (Book Fourteen)

The Sinful Suttons
Sutton's Spinster (Book One)
Sutton's Sins (Book Two)
Sutton's Surrender (Book Three)
Sutton's Seduction (Book Four)
Sutton's Scoundrel (Book Five)
Sutton's Scandal (Book Six)
Sutton's Secrets (Book Seven)

Rogue's Guild
Her Ruthless Duke (Book One)
Her Dangerous Beast (Book Two)
Her Wicked Rogue (Book 3)

Royals and Renegades
How to Love a Dangerous Rogue (Book One)

Sins and Scoundrels
Duke of Depravity
Prince of Persuasion
Marquess of Mayhem
Sarah
Earl of Every Sin
Duke of Debauchery
Viscount of Villainy

Sins and Scoundrels Box Set Collections
Volume 1
Volume 2

The Wicked Winters Box Set Collections
Collection 1
Collection 2
Collection 3
Collection 4

Wicked Husbands Box Set Collections
Volume 1
Volume 2

Stand-alone Novella
Lord of Pirates

CONTEMPORARY ROMANCE
Love's Second Chance
Reprieve (Book One)
Perfect Persuasion (Book Two)
Win My Love (Book Three)

Coastal Heat
Loved Up (Book One)

ABOUT THE AUTHOR

USA Today and Amazon bestselling author Scarlett Scott writes steamy Victorian and Regency romance with strong, intelligent heroines and sexy alpha heroes. She lives in Pennsylvania and Maryland with her Canadian husband, adorable identical twins, and two dogs.

A self-professed literary junkie and nerd, she loves reading anything, but especially romance novels, poetry, and Middle English verse. Catch up with her on her website https://scarlettscottauthor.com. Hearing from readers never fails to make her day.

Scarlett's complete book list and information about upcoming releases can be found at https://scarlettscottauthor.com.

Connect with Scarlett! You can find her here:
    Join Scarlett Scott's reader group on Facebook for early excerpts, giveaways, and a whole lot of fun!
    Sign up for her newsletter here
    https://www.tiktok.com/@authorscarlettscott

facebook.com/AuthorScarlettScott

x.com/scarscoromance

instagram.com/scarlettscottauthor

bookbub.com/authors/scarlett-scott

amazon.com/Scarlett-Scott/e/B004NW8N2I

pinterest.com/scarlettscott

Made in the USA
Monee, IL
08 February 2024

53181264R00094